Eloquent Blood

Audrey Lavin

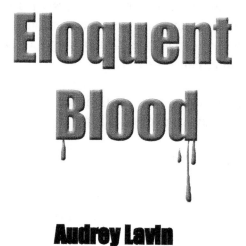

Eloquent Blood

Audrey Lavin

Daybreak Publishing, Ltd.
Canton, Ohio

Eloquent Blood

Printed in the United States of America on acid-free paper

Cover photo by:Nicole Bengiveno / The New York Times
Cover design and interior layout by: Dawn Kreutzberger
    Star Graphics and Web

ISBN: 0-9742233-4-4

    Library of Congress Cataloging-in-Publication Data

Lavin, Audrey A. P. (Audrey Ann Perlman)
  Eloquent blood / by Audrey Lavin.
      p. cm.
1. English teachers--Crimes against--Fiction. 2. Dog own-
ers--Crimes
against--Fiction. 3. Women college teachers--Fiction. 4.
Ohio--Fiction.
  I. Title.
  PS3612.A9443E46 2004
  813'.6--dc22
                                        2004022935

Dedication

This book is dedicated with love to my family:
Carl, Sr.
Locke, Maud, Krister, and David
Carl, Lauren, Austin, Seth, Carter, and Celeste
Franklin, Ann, Abby, Nat, and Liz
Douglas, Lisa, Simone, and Eleanor

Acknowledgements

With deep appreciation to all of those whose support and criticism have helped Mary Beth and Tony solve this mystery,

I thank you for your voices, thank you,
Your most sweet voices

(W. Shakespeare, Coriolanus)

To my family for emotional and editorial encouragement: Locke Bowman and Maud Lavin, Carl and Lauren S. Lavin, Franklin, Ann, and Abby Lavin, Douglas Lavin and Lisa Greenwald, and my favorite yea- and nay-sayer, Carl H. Lavin, Sr.

To the Wednesday Writing Workshop for shared laughter and informed analysis: Judi Christy, Bill Howland, David Manka, Lisa Muscarella, Ken Penix, Lyndon Sinclair, and Jim Swickard.

To many friends for suggestions that have been used to round characters and places.

To computer guru, Ernie Campbell, for his indispensable problem solving.

To Gemini Bicycle Center manager, Mike Ludwig, for his patient help in correlating bicycle and personality styles.

To owner, manager, and winemaker of Breitenbach Wine Cellars and Der MarketPlatz, Dalton (Duke) Bixler, for the generous sharing of his oenological wisdom (and wine tasting!)

To the late Stark County Probate Judge Robert D. (Bob) Horowitz for his knowledgeable explanations that kept me from making many procedural and technical errors.

I can personally lay claim to all errors that remain.

n.b. No dogs or other animals were harmed in the making of this novel

vi

Prologue

If once a man indulges himself in murder, very soon he comes to think little of robbing; and from robbing he comes next to drinking and Sabbath-breaking, and from that to incivility and procrastination.

"Murder Considered as One of the Fine Arts," 1827
Thomas DeQuincey

Chapter One

_"'Corridors of Power' –If a man hasn't a right to his
own cliché, who does?"_

C.P. Snow, Homecoming, 1956

❧

"Where is that damn cell phone?" I muttered as I excavated through stacks of ungraded papers on my desk. Ah, ha! Found it by the third ring, layered between the folds of the shearling coat I'd flung on my chair. I should have hung up my new coat after I unlocked the door to the English corridor and gracefully stumbled into my office. I should have stacked those student papers in some order to keep them from falling all over the floor, as they insisted on doing. Of course, my coat followed them when I yanked the phone out from under it.

"Good lord deliver us from battle and murder and from sudden death" were the words I heard half listening to the phone and half trying to organize the fallen papers with well-aimed kicks.

The chilling "deliver us from sudden death" litany isn't the usual greeting one expects to hear on picking up the phone. But it wasn't completely unusual as it was Tony calling. And part of Tony Bartlett's charm is that the unusual is usual for him. His quirky good looks combined with a rangy 6'2" frame don't detract from that charm either. He is different. What other Ph.D. would have quit a creative engineering research job in Princeton to follow me to mid-Ohio's Midfield College when I was hired as a leave replacement?

Tony had a second motivation for moving to what we thought would be peaceful Ohio. He also wanted some engineering release time to work on his opus magnum, *Bartlett's Better Book: Quotations You'll Use Every Day.* Boy, does he use them every day. He's been known to carry on whole conversations in the apt quotations that are part of his someday-to-be-published masterpiece.

But glancing underfoot at the 50 or so student essays that I was supposed to read made me impatient. I wasn't in the mood for Tony's relevant quotes, erudite or corny.

"Tony, stop it," I pleaded. "You used to be funny before you started to write that book of yours. Just stop using those long-way-around-the-barn citations every time you talk with me and tell me what you want. 'Good Lord deliver us" from what? Come on, Hon. I'm so behind in my work."

Besides, as if once weren't enough, I could hear every phrase he was saying in duplicate, so I complained some more. "Tony, either my office has developed a terrible echo or you're running down the hall and shouting into your cell phone at the same time."

"Good diagnosis, Dr. Goldberg. That's what I'm doing," yelled Tony almost simultaneously into the phone and into my office as he rushed through my open door, gesticulating wildly with one hand while waving his cell phone in the direction of his ear with the other. "I started to call you from Gary's office, Mary Beth, but I had to make sure you knew I was serious."

He stopped waving his right arm so he could use it to grab me by the shoulder without relinquishing the cell phone appendage attached to his left. While pushing me along, he seemed to think he was explaining something about having called for an ambulance. I admit that I was more concerned about the dirt he was transferring from his hand to my pink cashmere sweater than what he was saying, but I let him propel me down the English department's corridor in Loomis Hall. "At least I didn't say, 'murder most foul,'" he roared into the phone he was still holding in his left hand while continuing to drag me along with his right.

I thought Tony was trying to steer me down the stairs and out of the building, so I was surprised when he pulled me up short at Gary Hake's office, only two cells down from mine. My surprise turned to disbelief-then horror-as I looked into what is normally the most boring and well-ordered office in the department. Usually every item from pencils to chairs is rigidly in place, a surface manifestation of Gary's almost frightening need for control. But what I saw was the antithesis of control.

Tony gasped something directly at me: "Doesn't it look like murderS most foul?" He added in a somewhat calmer voice, "Look. Krypto is dead. Mygod, Mary Beth, can't you see? That's a corkscrew sticking out of her throat. She's murdered just like a person. It's surreal."

In spite of the shock, I couldn't keep myself from saying, "What do you mean just like a person? There's a real person lying here too. He's dead too, isn't he?" The body was prone and contorted, but I recognized the back of the well-shaped head, the black, tightly curled hair. I saw the outstretched dark-skinned hand. I knew . . . .

"Yes. Yes. It's Les." Tony knelt down on the floor next to the body, adding blood to the grease and other debris staining his work jeans. He felt for what we both realized would be a non-existent pulse and explained, "I called the ambulance. I hoped he was still alive, but he's as dead as, as dead as . . . Krypto is. What in the world were they doing here together? Les doesn't . . . didn't . . . even like Border collies or any dogs. And why would they get themselves killed in Gary's office?"

"Where would you suggest they get themselves killed, Tony?" I could hear my voice rising an octave in out-of-control sarcasm. "Anyway, that's hardly the question now, is it?"

Tony reached out to comfort me, but he couldn't stop my shivering. His hands were as cold as mine were; it was that plunge of blood pressure unexpected horror brings on.

My stomach was churning so, it was all I could do to control myself and not retch. I forced my stomach into something approaching normalcy by thinking how embarrassed I'd be if I threw up and ruined all of the evidence. Then I had another worry: How could I be so shallow as to be concerned about embarrassing myself at a time like this?

All of it-the cold, the trauma, and the literally gut-wrenching sadness converted my response to my love and best friend into an irrational monologue.

"What could they be doing here? Krypto's our official mascot. She has entrée to every office. Why wouldn't she be here? Except this all happened after hours." Close to hysterical, I rapidly asked and answered my own questions.

"You do have a good question, Mary Beth. What was Les doing in Gary's office? Gary's is an invitation-only office."

I knew that. And I knew that Les had his own desk along with the other part-timers in the Adjunct Office at the other end of the hall. As a part-timer, he doesn't rate a key to the corridor or to offices.

Tony was still talking, as much to himself as to me, "Krypto couldn't have wagged the doors open. Someone had to have let them both in."

I was reeling with emotion and again spoke more sharply than I intended, "Don't try to answer me through that cell phone while we're practically on top of each other. Call the ambulance again. Call the sheriff."

"What'll we say?" The question showed how upset Tony was. In our three years together, he had never before asked me that question

"What'll we say? Tony, honey, whatever you say, DON'T use any of your collection of quotations. Save them for your *Bartlett's Better Book.*"

"But, Mary Beth," he protested, "I was just coming up to see you. Now I've got to explain all of this to the police? All I did was look into Gary's office as I passed by. The door was open! You know that S.O.B. is the only one who always keeps his door closed. And doesn't even post any *New Yorker* cartoons on it. When I looked in, I saw Krypto with, I couldn't believe it-I still can't believe it-a corkscrew in her neck. Of course I looked in further. Blood on the floor. And that bloody paperweight on the desk. It must have been the murder weapon used on Les. Oh, talking about it is making me sick. And staying here is worse. That moldering death smell is on the edge of - of putrescence, that's what. Move into the hall. Please. Les was a nice guy, but I really love . . . loved Krypto." Tony staggered forward. He compensated for almost fainting with a quick jerk backward, and supported himself against Gary's file cabinet.

I knew that as much as he loved Krypto, Tony wasn't heartless. He loved his fellow man and woman, too, at least as much as the next guy does, but as a newcomer to Midfield he had found it much easier to make friends with Krypto than with Les.

I had settled into my digs a month before Tony could finish his project with the Center for Information Systems

Research and leave Princeton to be with me. My arrival on campus coincided with Les Delaney's, so the two of us were paired off as the newcomers on the block when the fall semester started. Besides arriving at Midfield at the same time, Les and I had two other ambitions and experiences in common: the frantic desire to break into the old boys' network that ruled the English department and the failure to do so. Underlying other adjustments, I suspect, is that in this small Midwestern town, we were both different, 'the other.' All by myself, I perceptibly changed the percentage of Jews in Midfield just as Les changed the percentage of African-Americans. So we were close colleagues if not really friends. I had tried. Tony and I had invited Les and his girlfriend over for a few unreciprocated Sunday night suppers. Well, I decided, I was busy, too, and wouldn't push for friendship. But lately Les had seemed friendlier and upbeat, stopping at my office to talk about the future instead of giving me an update on his usual health and career problems.

Now suddenly, horribly, he was dead. With all of Les's hypo-chondriac complaints and real allergies, I wouldn't have been surprised if he had died from poison ivy or peanut butter, but not murder. As almost co-discoverer of the bodies, it was my immediate responsibility to do something, at least to notify members of the English department. "Look, Tony," I said, "while you're calling the police, I'll go back to my office and call Gary. Whatever happened, it happened in his office. His department. But we don't want to use his phone, and, what do they say, 'contaminate the crime scene.' What kind of a crime scene is this anyway? Did you ever have a drink with Gary in his office? Do you know if that's his corkscrew getting all bloody in Krypto's neck?"

"Wait. Where will you call him? You can't call him in his office. That's where we are. And obviously he's not." Tony moved from the file cabinet's support to walk a bit unsteadily across the room and pointed over my head. "He's not in class either. Here are his hours, posted right on the wall behind you. Let's see. Last class is over at 4 p.m. today. Now it's almost 5 p.m."

"You're right, Tony. He should be in the lounge getting ready for the weekly department meeting. I'll call there. That's the easy call. Someone else will have to call Les's girlfriend Margarita. I can't do it. Honey, I just can't do it."

Tony and I had sometimes felt isolated, out of the loop, at Midfield Campus College during our two months together in Ohio. But our discovery of the bodies, the phone calls, and the subsequent arrival of the police, ambulance, and hangers-on quickly put a stop to that. Now, by the end of October, we were where we thought we had wanted to be at the beginning of September, in the middle of things. But in the middle of a murder? The middle of a muddle? Not quite the academic centrality I had been aiming for.

For most of my first semester's teaching at Midfield, I know that everyone thought of me as the new 'temp' at the College even though Gary Hake and Co. had recruited me because of my (beginning) national reputation. My investigations of the ways Edward Morgan Forster used external patterns and internal rhythms in his novels had created an almost fiery national partisanship among literary critics.

But at Midfield, the academic environment was chilly. I began to think I had made a mistake in coming to Ohio. Tony said that any discomfort was just my paranoia and started to describe me and my attitude with Marianne Moore's, "water buffaloes, neurasthenic-even murderous." Then I was assigned that office about as far from the department as possible, down in the basement of Midfield College's Buckeye Library. It's affectionately called "The Buck," but in those first few weeks, I didn't share in that affection. Tony tried to restore my morale by telling me that I was as clever and good looking as a Ph.D. had a right to be. Even on my worst bad hair days, he assured me, I really didn't look like an endangered buffalo though I was starting to growl like one. Unfortunately I wasn't paranoid or neurasthenic; I was just being treated like someone at the bottom of the hierarchy. I couldn't get any of the good old boys interested in mentoring me either. Though Charlie Volstadt made it apparent that if it weren't for Tony, some 'mentoring' might be forthcoming from his corner.

Then last week I was 'promoted' from my English department outpost. I was no longer banished to the basement of the Buck. When Administration borrowed Roger Christian from the English department for another year to work in Community Relations, my office was moved to his former space in Loomis Hall. A space which happened to be right next to Charlie Volstadt's office. More problems?

I was glad that during those first couple of weeks of feeling low I hadn't pitched my wildly vining wandering Jew, summer's drying hydrangeas, the great American lit. posters I had collected over the years -my nesting materials. I proudly taped my favorite *New Yorker* cartoon by Mankoff on my new office door, the cartoon that shows a woman in bed saying to the man next to her, "Why, you're right. Tonight isn't reading night, tonight is sex night." One of my students had labeled the couple "Mary Beth" and "Tony", reflecting the informal rapport I've achieved with the kids. But I still feel only tenuously connected to my colleagues. Even though officially I'm a Visiting Professor, and I love the title, it's obvious that socially and academically I continue to be the new 'Temp.'

Instead of trying harder to integrate myself into the department, I had been on a self-pitying roll that built from mild self-complaints to repeated internal fuming. On the other hand, I wasn't as overtly cranky as some. As a two-year leave replacement, I wasn't up for tenure. I've seen the fear of not getting it, or worse, the fear of losing tenure, change an almost-normally benign professor to an alien horror from *Men in Black III*. I doubt if I were threatened by loss of tenure I'd start emulating Machiavelli instead of preparing to teach him, but who knows?

I thought of an addition to my list of complaints: the reaction when I introduce Tony to my colleagues at M.C.C., Tony, a guy who works with his hands (gasp!) at the local bicycle repair shop and who wears genuinely dirty jeans. Subtly and oh, so politely we're placed outside of the intellectual hierarchy, even by all of my politically correct colleagues who love the working man in the abstract. The next time I introduce Tony to anyone, I'm going to start right out with his advanced engineering degree from M.I.T. no matter how crude it sounds. When I start with his name and Midfield job, no one stays around long enough for me to work his information systems research or his academic credentials into the conversation. Or maybe they're not as fascinated by bicycle gear ratios as Tony is.

Chapter Two

"It is by presence of mind in untried emergencies that the natural metal of a man <or woman> is tested."

James Russell Lowell, "Abraham Lincoln," 1864

❧

A small campus in a small town does have some advantages. While I was still making the necessary telephone calls, the Basic Life Support ambulance arrived with a paramedic, his CPR certified driver, and a volunteer. The two professionals made a determination of death and were out of there, leaving only the volunteer to wait for the police and turn what was now legally a crime scene over to them.

Within five minutes of completing our phone calls, members of the English department-driven by various motivations from curiosity about the crimes to compassion for the victims to concern for their own positions-arrived on the scene.

Within ten minutes the first member of Midfield's diminutive police force, Deputy Dwayne Miller, arrived.

"10-23. Stand by." he announced. "I'm here. I'm in charge."

He officiously collected nearby briefcases as possible carriers of evidence. "10-26," he explained, "I'm doing cop work." Dwayne Miller loves being a policeman, even though he can't seem to memorize the Buckeye State's Sheriff's Code and still uses his old CB lingo.

Some of the briefcases did look splattered. But was that blood on them or just plain dirt? My colleagues indulge in a reverse snobbism that causes each professor to claim his is the most worn, the oldest briefcase. A beat-up briefcase is local badge of honor.

Deputy Miller carefully numbered each case and placed them one by one on the rug in Gary's office, then floundered, obviously wondering what to do next. Fortunately he didn't have to decide. His arrival and securing of the briefcase evidence was almost immediately followed by the appearance on the scene of Seth Yoder, the town's sheriff/detective, who decisively took charge of what was by then a hullabaloo. So much was going on that for a while I lost Tony in the commotion.

Give or take another five minutes and the Campus Patrol, including my friend and student, Patrol Officer Amos Hershberger, added three more to the crowd. It meant a lot to me to see a familiar and official face. But offices don't expand and Amos and colleagues were left bulging out of Gary's office, overflowing into the corridor of what the English department considers its domain.

The detective in charge, known as Just-call-me-Seth

Yoder, is in fact Midfield's only detective. He first took a few good Midwestern minutes to thank Tony and me for what he called our "surprisingly coherent" phone calls to him, the ambulance, and members of the English department. He explained that many people react to horror with a kind of defense mechanism that allows them to temporarily continue with their normal activities as we had done, but we should expect a strong counter-reaction. Almost patting me on the head, he assured us that delayed hysteria was quite common after traumatic incidents. Then, moving quickly to his official mode, he declared Stew's office, the one between Gary's and mine, the Control Room. Seth told us he was acting on his preferred (and previously unpracticed) theory that time and space proximity to the crime would hasten the solution. Tony and I watched, clutching each other's hands, as he quickly ordered Deputy Miller and the Campus Patrol to put the yellow crime scene tape in place; asked for a list of all who used the Hall, especially full and part-time department members; and announced he would take on the responsibility of notifying Les's parents, the Delaneys, and Les's girlfriend Margarita Maria Berenguer. Those calls were responsibilities I had planned to take on and was happy to relinquish. It was horrible enough seeing the dead; I dreaded having to talk to the living about them.

When questioned, I explained what I had considered my obligation to talk with the Delaneys and Margarita to Officer Yoder. "Not 'Officer Yoder.' Just call me Seth," he predictably admonished. He didn't question either Tony or me for any length of time in Stew's office. This was just a preliminary interview. And the only personal evidence that he took was my dearly beloved badge of professionalism, my leather briefcase. It joined the stack of vaguely familiar ones Miller had collected and originally left in Gary's office. They were now neatly arranged according to Miller's number code next to "his" desk, eminently domained from Stew. I was beginning to have the delayed reaction of frustration and emotion that Seth had warned me about, so I think he wanted me out of there just as much as I wanted to be out of there.

Later everyone told me that when I saw the child-sized stretcher being carried in for her body, I screamed, "Why? Why Krypto?" My screams jolted the rest of the staff soberly milling around in the corridor waiting their turns to be questioned by members of the police force. And I don't even remember calling out. I can only recall the feeling of my face and stomach muscles tightening with horror.

"Why not go home and get some sleep, 'sleep of the innocent.' It really will make you feel better," Tony quieted me, not so far from a breakdown himself. He was more aware than I was that the next day might bring further, and more official, interrogations. Plus, I think he was beginning to feel as if he were guilty, just because he was standing around in his blood-stained jeans. People were beginning to look at him.

Tony's caring made me smile even under the circumstances, demonstrating that screams aren't the only cathartic release available. As I wiped my eyes and straightened my sweater, I said, "'There's a cure for everything,' isn't there, 'except death.'" I caught myself. "Oh, damn it, Tony. I'm beginning to talk in quotations-as if I were you."

Chapter Three

"He who would distinguish the true from the false must have an adequate idea of what is true and false."

Spinoza, Ethics, 1677

୨ৱ

Tony saw me safely to my house, a very ordinary white frame house that I'd been extraordinarily lucky to find. It's in the high-rent district right at the edge of campus, tucked between two circa 1860s homes, architectural stars of the Midfield Heritage Association. I'm close enough to Loomis Hall to run home between classes and pick up a paper if I'd ever forget one, so it took no time at all for Tony to walk me home. It was surprisingly consoling to walk up the familiar thirty-foot concrete path that leads from the sidewalk to my porch steps. It was reassuring to see my unchained Raleigh Comfort bike on the green porch and to remember that here in the town of Midfield no one locks bicycles. We trust each other. Who had Les trusted? Who had given Krypto her last pat? Who would she have been able to sniff out? I tried to shake away the devastating image of the dead bodies.

Tony watched me open the door, gave me an extra hug, and rushed back to Loomis to find out what he could do to be of help. I fell asleep immediately in my favorite arm chair with Grandma Fanny's afghan wrapped warmly around me. Funny, I had hated that afghan when Grandma Fanny made it and gave it to me. What nine-year-old girl would want her birthday gift to be a hand-crocheted afghan with huge pink roses all over it? Now that Grandma is gone, it is my most prized possession. Whether it was due to the warmth of the afghan or a need to retreat and an attempt to erase the murders, I slept so deeply that Tony had to awaken me to put me to bed later that night.

While fixing our midnight hot cocoas, he brought me up to date. When he got back to Loomis, the same group was still aimlessly moving around the English department offices and corridor in a shocked patternless drift of stops and starts. Trying to discover the center of activity, Tony found himself pushed into a position between Gary Hake and Stew Jones who were discussing when they had last seen Les. Had he said anything significant? Had he been unduly agitated about something? They were too agitated themselves to remember.

Their self-questioning was interrupted by Deputy Dwayne Miller's striding importantly into the corridor. As usual he was wearing his well-pressed khaki deputy's uniform, topped with his trademark Cleveland Indians baseball cap-brim forward this evening to show respect. Miller put the two briefcases he was carrying on the floor and dramatically closed the door behind him, the door to what had been Stew's office and was now the sheriff's. The plan was to keep the protected crime scene in Gary's office closed to the public for the duration of the investigation and to use Stew's office next to it as Crime Central. Someone had already taped a cardboard sign on Gary's office door with "CRIME SCENE" printed on it in big red felt-tipped letters. Deputy Dwayne stood in the corridor with the "CRIME SCENE" sign as backdrop. Arms crossed over his chest; he was at the ready to address the group. As he stood there waiting, all became silent. Tony said it really was that wave of silence you read about. The wave started with those who had been standing and talking close to Miller and gradually extended to the door at the end of the corridor.

When Deputy Miller felt he had command of the situation, he held aloft the two briefcases he had carried out of the office. "I think we've solved this here little murder before we start," he said in his Hollywood version of law enforcement language. "See these here two cases?" He almost waved them.

"He must do a lot of weight training," Tony interjected when telling me the story. "Those briefcases are both leather and filled with books as well as papers," he explained.

Everyone turned to look up at the sinister briefcases. "This 'un," Miller went on, "has initials on it 'G. H. H.,' so we know it belongs to Gary H. Hake and that's a darn good thing for you, Professor Hake, whoever you are."

"I'm right here, *sir*," Gary bristled. "Any accusations you have to make, you'd better make them directly to me. Unless you would prefer my attorney, *sir*."

"10-2. Good. I said it's a good thing, Professor Hake. Don't get your boils all riled up and pussing there or you won't be able to sit down again. It's a good thing it's your briefcase because threads from your rug can easily be seen on the side and bottom of it," and he pulled off a few blue fibers to illustrate his point.

"But that's O.K.," he said negating Gary's angry look and aggressive step forward.

Stew broke the tension, nervously yelling out, "Can a Hake be a red herring?-or is that too fishy a pun?"

"As usual Stew was inappropriate, but funny," Tony judged, commenting on his report. He returned to his tale of the night's adventure by quoting Deputy Miller's speech:

"I'm trying to tell you that's O.K., sir, because it's your office and we would expect to find fibers from your rug on your possessions. But this second briefcase I looked at," and Dwayne more violently waved the case in his left hand. "This 'un has threads, too. Whose bag is this? Any fool can see that the perp entered the office where the murder took place and put this down on the rug when he went after the victim, victims that is. O.K., who's the owner? I want him there when I go through the case and when I remove threads for forensic investigation, which we don't even need except for the trial, 'cause like I said, any fool can plainly see these rug fibers are from Mr. Hake's rug. No boltin' for the door anyone. We've got it covered." His threatening waves of the hand were unnecessary. Except for curious turns of heads, no one was moving.

Tony smiled and gently teased me again about a fan of mine who had been part of the evening's activities, "Sure enough, your good pal, Amos, and another rent-a-cop were barring the exit. They managed to look the way they probably felt, foolish and tough at the same time."

Stew, who was still on Tony's left, elbowed his way forward not noticing or caring who he bruised as he realized the full exultation of starring in his personal drama.

"I lay claim to that briefcase and all of the goods therein," he intoned, as if reading from the same poor Hollywood script that Deputy Dwayne was following. Stew being Stew, he added, "I think your analysis of the case is more off the wall than off the rug."

Meanwhile, that quiet guy who interviewed us, the one who says, "Just call me Seth" all the time, came out of the office and whispered something into Dwayne's ear. The more he whispered, the more Dwayne kept pulling the peak of his cap up and down in a signal that ranged between a salute and a nod of affirmation. Tony reported that no one knew what was going on when they both disappeared back into Command Central, the command post that had been Stew's office just a few hours earlier. Stew seemed almost disappointed. He had been so ready to do battle for his honor. He knew darn well that the threads on his briefcase had nothing to do with murder and he was proud and prepped to prove it.

An hour or so later, those who had stayed on learned that Stew was absolutely right. Every single one of the briefcases collected as evidence had fibers from Gary's rug on them. Why? Because the first officer on the scene, Deputy Dwayne Miller, whose resume consists of a list of the speeding tickets he's issued, had collected all of the briefcases and carefully stored them in Gary's office on Gary's rug!

I felt guilty when I laughed at this story until Tony reminded me that I wasn't the only one to mix the emotions of amusement and grief. "Proverbs," he reminded me, "says, 'Even in laughter the heart is sorrowful.'"

More generous than I am, Tony was ready to excuse Dwayne. "Miller's well intended," he explained, "but he's obviously never before worked even a minor homicide, if there is such a thing, let alone a double one."

Tony smothered a yawn. By now it was way after midnight of what had been an astoundingly intense day. "Excuse me. I guess I'm a little tired, Mary Babe, but speaking of mixed emotions and Midfield's police force, I have a message for you. Your rent-a-cop friend Amos, said to say 'hey' and to let him know if you needed anything, anything at all. I'm right. He does have a thing for you."

Later that night, still awake and keeping ourselves that way by going over and over details, Tony and I realized that

Dwayne's too-fast-on-the-draw accusation of Stew must have triggered Sheriff Seth Yoder's announcement that as the community's chief law enforcement officer, he alone would take active charge of the investigation.

Chapter Four

*"Economists report that a college education adds many
thousands of dollars to a man's lifetime income—which
he then spends sending his son to college."*

Bill Vaughn, 1971

&

Murders don't take place at Midfield Campus College,
founded and forgotten by the Presbyterian Synod. Many
say that nothing takes place on this bucolic campus in
postcard-pretty Midfield, Ohio. The College had quickly
lived down the intellectual thrust inherent in its 1826
self-given title "the Yale of the West." Today the highest
level of excitement is the occasional skirmish between
administration and students when every few years some new,
enterprising sophomore tries to manufacture and sell T-shirts
with "McCollege" emblazoned on a background that looks
suspiciously like golden arches. The administration and
Board of Trustees consider this an inappropriate and undigni-

fied symbol for the college. But in all campus references, except those emanating from the administrative offices, "McCollege" supercedes the "M.C.C." official logo. Some of the more daring women students invite a closer inspection of the T-shirt background, a giggling inspection, most often by their male counterparts, that clearly shows the pseudo arches to be a blurred photograph of two campus towers. Administration can win the T-shirt battle by prohibiting sales in the campus bookstore, but they can't win the McCollege war. The students, in this skirmish more sophisticated than the administration, like to joke of their meaty, quality controlled education, topped with the sesame seeds of a few politically correct literature and women's studies courses.

Midfield's classes are held and students are housed in quadrangles of buildings that do their best to look British. "Cover any thing not moving with ivy" had been somebody's mid-Ohio interpretation of Oxford and Cambridge architecture. "Throw in arches and larches," an anonymous contributor had added, and an attractively inauthentic campus of antiqued buildings and courtyards was the result.

Crimes at the College are perceived to be non-U and non-existent. Many in administration know of the rape that had occurred on campus six years earlier, for example, but that had been successfully hushed up. The minor crime of petty theft was common and commonly ignored except for the Dean of Students' constant admonition to keep doors locked. Students from small towns in the Heartland stylishly display fistfuls of keys hanging from back pockets of jeans, an unconscious 21st century version of the chatelaines that they find so esoteric in required departmental readings. Usually the only one that works is that proudly displayed car key, so tapes and small appliances are easily, albeit illegally, moved from one unlocked dorm room to another. This is why members of the English department are so careful about locking up. In the dorms, however, no one has to face the rejection implicit in asking to borrow something. Whatever is needed is casually taken. The Dean didn't even bother to add Midfield Campus's pilfering rate to last year's national burglary total of 212 for four-year private colleges. But Les's death was another story and would certainly appear in the data base for college crime statistics. Unfortunately, Les's claim to immortality would not be realized in his dream of a published thesis. It would be found instead at the federal Web site <http://ope.ed.gov/security>.

Not having any experience in how to react to a murder, the College did not formally do so except for a brief, and typically understated, press release of regret. The document had been carefully crafted by College President Fairchild Bender (Oh, the students loved that name!) and his Vice President of Community Relations, Caroline Mossberg, so that it performed triple duty: a condolence note to Mr. and Mrs. Delaney, Les's parents; a reassurance to students when published in the weekly edition of the Campus Speaker; and a "we're in control-classes as usual" message to the town's Midfield Repository and the public at large, if the public at large should notice. The first and last sentences of the press package, whether pertinent or not, seem to have been used for every public announcement in living memory. The boilerplate release started, "The terrible events of yesterday surprised and sorrowed us all. Even when there is a long lead time, such a critical event marks a significant change and challenge to a college." It ended, "We have academically talented students, outstanding faculty, staff, and alumni, an always improving campus, a balanced budget, support of the community, and generous donors. We have a commitment to excellence in all that we do, and we have the people who can make sure that we achieve that standard. These resources give us good reason for pride and confidence as we move ahead toward the future." Sandwiched between this not-quite logical introduction and trite conclusion was the succinct tribute to Les.

Particular consideration had been given to the wording of the concise Les insert because of his African-American heritage, as we say around here. It's difficult enough to recruit blacks to study or teach at Midfield without getting word out about their being murdered on the job. It's not that prospective students are informed enough to know that Ohio lags behind the rest of the country in its acceptance of diversity or that Ohio's Hate Crime Law has a serious drafting error: assault is omitted. No, the reason many minority students don't apply is that the traditional campus tour makes it visually apparent that no critical mass of any ethnic minority group studies here.

The sharp on-line editor of the *Campus Speaker*, more attuned to today's communication conventions than are Bender and Mossberg, had taken it on himself late Monday afternoon to notify all students by email. Bender's letter of regret, then, was anti-climactic and generally un-read.

Meanwhile, each of the old-guard members of the English department-after all, it was THEIR crime-had composed an appropriate 'spontaneous' comment on the case, complete with footnotes and a convenient bibliography that listed anything he had ever published. By an unspoken consensus, it was deemed inappropriate to list days available for interviews-those national interviews that were never requested.

With the need for some type of conclusion uppermost in its collective mind, Administration planned a memorial service at the non-denominational (Jews and Muslims weren't supposed to notice the two storey-high cross on the outside wall) chapel for Tuesday morning.

On the way to chapel, I went to my office for the first time since the murders. Was that less than twenty-four hours ago? When I closed the door, I was startled to see Les's beige cardigan hanging on the hook. He must have left it when he stopped in to gossip on Saturday morning. It still smelled slightly of Ralph Lauren's Polo Blue. Les couldn't smell the difference between a designer and a drugstore brand, but others could, and he liked the effect of wearing an expensive cologne. I used to laugh at this affectation, but suddenly it was an endearing feature. It hit me. Les was a person. Like the rest of us, he wanted to be noticed, to be loved. His parents and Margarita loved him. I bent to inhale the remnants of Ralph Lauren's Polo again. Les was my colleague. I owed him. I stuffed the sweater into my old, back-up briefcase and hurried on to chapel.

During the service, the murder itself was passed over so quickly that at the time I didn't realize it was never fully acknowledged. Five members of the college community took part in the ceremony. The school chaplain opened with a prayer. He was followed by President Bender, who gave the official funeral oration. Bender announced Les's untimely death as the result of a contusion, due to blunt force trauma, making it sound almost as if Les had hit himself on the head. He closed his portion of the service by saying, "The dead can't speak for themselves. Only we can speak for them," and proceeded to tell of Les's strong devotion to Midfield Campus College, the College's commitment to excellence, and his own 'synergistic vision.'

"Now Vice President Mossberg," he continued "will tell you about your college's plan to prevent the reoccurrence of the incident that has caused unease on our peaceful campus."

Caroline Mossberg took the podium. Her demeanor was grave. "I'm sorry to have to follow these beautiful prayers and speeches with some announcements. First let me say, my heart goes out to the Delaneys and to all of Les's other friends who are here today." She looked embarrassed, as well she should, when she announced that S.O.S. whistles were now being distributed at no cost to all women and men students who lived on campus. They could be picked up at the Wellness Center.

"Dr. Bender has asked me to inform you," she persevered, reading now from Bender's announcement, "that these safety whistles are being distributed even though they are not required by the National Campus Security Policy, better known as the Jeanne Clery Act. Dr. Bender adds that your college is required to provide crime information to members of the campus community, but in the Midfield Campus College tradition, we have gone beyond what is required to provide each of you with a personal safety device at absolutely no charge." Caroline wiped her brow, with added embarrassment, I'm sure, and sat down.

As Chair of Les's department, Gary was the natural choice as eulogist. He spoke of Les's graduate studies and his teaching assignments. He was very matter of fact. When Curt Perlis from Chemistry mildly criticized him later by saying, "your eulogy wasn't exactly a ringing endorsement," Gary replied, "It wasn't meant to be. Les didn't exactly add scholarly heft to the department."

The eulogy was followed by one of Les's Comp. students giving a tearful memory of Les in class. All of us attending the service concluded it by joining together to recite the Lord's Prayer.

As soon as the service was over, I noted to myself that classes, meetings, academic intrigues, and facetious remarks followed their usual patterns. In fact, on the way out of Chapel, Stew whispered to me—tastefully, "Despite the cost of living, do you notice how popular it still seems?" Over the top. Under the top! That joke had been buried years ago. What was the matter with me? Stew was contagious. I pulled myself together.

I had been somewhat interested in solving the murder as an intellectual puzzle, but the public callousness displayed by Bender, Hake, Stewart, et al made me determined to remind them that Les was a real person, killed by someone who might even be on our campus. I thought of that beige cardigan in my brief case, still smelling of Ralph Lauren's Polo Blue. I made a private resolution to talk about Les.

The students in my Forster class appreciated my bringing up the subject. They needed to talk about it, too. Although the day's assignment was on *A Room with a View*, I made a quick switch by passing out copies of Forster's essay, "A New Novelist." I high-lighted his words, "It is for a voyage into solitude that man was created. The soul like the body voyages at her own risk." We discussed Les's complete solitude-death-and segued to the type of social solitude Lucy in *A Room* is threatened with when she goes against society and chooses George.

Class discussion kept circling around and coming back to Les's death. The more I talked about it in class, the more I felt that I owed it to Les to help find his murderer; I owed it to myself; and I certainly owed it to those who were almost conspiring in a societal cover-up of the 'unhappy occurrence.' I might have been turning myself into The Masked Crusader, but at least my emotions were genuine.

I thought again of that beige cardigan.

How hard could detecting be, I asked myself. It must be something like academic research, and I'm very good at that.

The place to start looking for clues was student gossip. For the first time in academic history, we members of the English department were interesting people to the students. Where else would the murderer come from? Not just "Who dun it?" but rather, "Which one of them do you think dun it?" was the question posed by English majors, minors, and those who could still remember their profs from Freshman Comp. Oops. There I go again. I corrected myself. First year comp. No one seemed to think that the crime was racially motivated. Even the college's few radicals who had drifted into the Black Studies and Women's Studies departments-and who saw their raison d'être as ruckus raising whenever possible-were pretty subdued at the seriousness of the situation.

But by mid-afternoon, student protestors were back on track. It was a bright, sunny autumnal day made more for marching than for sitting in classes listening to boring profs drone on. By afternoon, the students were well supplied with the newly dispersed warning whistles, which they blew as they marched in cadence.

Most students had cared deeply for Krypto. A darling photograph of her had been digitally enlarged, copied, and expanded into 20 or 30 black and white placards. Most of the posters carried the picture with the words, "Find Krypto's killer."   But there were others clearly based on materials from People for the Ethical Treatment of Animals. I assume it was the Spanish majors who were raising the signs that said, "Si, Se Puede" (the name of the PETA award in honor of Cesar Chavez). Others borrowed from PETA's official title, and carried SETA posters, declaring themselves to be "Students for the Ethical Treatment of Animals." Maybe these signs weren't specifically on target, but they added to the general feeling of protest and outrage felt on campus. Some students, late arrivals and more emotionally off-track, carried their own home-made posters, "Remember the Animal's Agenda," "Dump the Iditarod," and the ubiquitous "No Math Requirements!"

Chapter Five

"A narrow compass! and yet there
Dwelt all that's good and all that's fair."

Edmund Waller 1606-1687

ॐ

The student protest and my own growing emotional involvement with the case made the climate of business as usual on campus seem heartless to me. While I was determined to honor Les by broadening my priorities to include solving his murder, the only change made by the department was one of necessity: to change the regular meeting to Tuesday afternoon instead of Monday.

Just before that rescheduled gathering of the English Professorial tribe, I felt an urgent need to bask in the security of Tony. Besides, I like to hug Tony. I like to feel his strength. I like to feel the muscles of his back. The thoughts of physically unwinding with him, even if it wasn't going to be in bed, were enough to speed up my walk toward the bike shop where he worked. I almost ran as I detoured to Bob's Superbikes ("We Recycle Cycles") on the way to the Faculty Lounge. I stopped only to pick up some trash, a discarded placard from the earlier student demonstration for Krypto. This one commanded, "Beat Ohio State. Not Seals." Appropriate? No. But I was still smiling over it as I entered the shop. The eponymous Bob greeted me with a complicated wave. I deciphered its meaning as half, "Hey, Mary Beth" and half, "Wait a second." Bob conducts whatever business he can in the front of the store. He makes himself as visible as possible to customers. Seeing the owner on hand to solve problems is reassuring to both novice and semi-pro cyclists. This time he was talking on the phone to an unresponsive supplier who again was behind in shipments. An impatient customer stood facing him, egging him on. Typically, she wanted her bike yesterday. As I passed the impatient student, I could see she was one of my star pupils, Alice Ming. I got a "Hi, Dr. G." from her, accompanied with a knowing smile. My students track Tony's and my relationship as if they were following a telenovella. Try to keep anything quiet on this campus.

Bob hung up and made some conventional remarks about Les Delaney's death. I wasn't aware that Bob knew Les, but, hey, this is small-town Ohio. I was warned before I came to always keep my dresser drawers neat! I waited.

"Mary Beth, would you spread the word, please. I now have a new Cannondale that I'd like to get rid of. It's already been shipped, should be here tomorrow, and will have a 'SALE' sign on it as soon as it's unpacked. I'm sure Les's estate won't want it."

"Les's estate? What are you talking about, Bob?"

"Well, he ordered and put down a payment on this Cannondale. That's one expensive bike. Plus, he ordered it custom painted-in your school colors, too. What am I supposed to do with a purple and white bike? I'd like to get rid of it without taking too much of a loss. I'm just lucky I talked him out of having his name signatured on it. Then I'd never sell it. I'm asking everyone to spread the word."

"I'll try, Bob," I assured him. "If you'll give me some flyers with a description of the bike, I'll put them up on campus bulletin boards for you, though I'm sure Tony knows more bikers than I do."

I thought about the Cannondale. If Les had ordered an expensive bike, custom painted in M.C.C's school colors, he must have expected (A) a promotion with a real salary increase and (B) that the promotion was going to be permanent. He was planning to stay at Midfield. Where else could he ride a purple and white bicycle and not feel silly?

While trying to figure out who had promised Les a tenured position (Roger? Stew?), I skirted boxes of newly arrived winter ski equipment. Entrepreneur Bob filled in his slow biking months with minor ski sales. No wonder he wanted to get rid of the one of a kind and out of season Cannondale. His selection of comfort bikes were already on sale and took up the entrance wall. The real cycling enthusiasts had to walk further back to find specialty bikes, trail or racing bikes.

Seeking Tony, I followed the sales path Bob had arranged among racks of jackets. The cycling jerseys hanging on the wall tempted me for a minute. Tony and I were talking about taking a two-day trip in Ohio's wine country. I could use a jacket and some gear. But I didn't have a minute. I wanted to see Tony now and I had to get to the department meeting.

Some customers thought Bob overstocked. Not I. I didn't feel closed-in walking down the narrow aisle left by all of the floor racks and wall racks loaded with bicycles, bicycle helmets, bicycle seats, and other accessories. The bicycles hanging, front wheels angled down, from either side of the ceilings made me think I was at West Point with the bikes acting as equivalents of crossed swords at a special ceremony. What ceremony? A wedding? A wedding in a bike shop? Stop that, Mary Beth Goldberg. Give this relationship a little more time.

A few more steps and I came to where the noticeably clean industrial carpeting stopped. This was Bob's way of separating the sales from the work area. From here to the back door was a stained concrete floor presided over by Tony, wearing his uniform, a black bib apron over black jeans and turtleneck. Some grease always escaped the confines of the aprons Bob issued, but they were essentially protective.

Tony was standing behind his work station adjusting the derailleurs to improve shifting on a customer's bike. Next to him was his personal repair stand, which includes a can of his secret ingredient, Pam No Stick Cooking Spray, to fix bicycle chains that are stuck. This is where he works on his semi-permanent project, re-equipping his Paramount with Campognola parts. He raised his arm in a surprised greeting almost hitting himself, almost hitting me, with the Park tri-Allen wrench he was using. He quickly put the wrench down on an improvised table made up of boxes of biking shoes that had been moved from sales to make room for the ski display.

"Hey, Mary Best," he said, still involved with his work. "It's been a fun work day today and you're making it even better. Folks usually come in for a regular cheap-o $30-$35 bike tune-up. Pretty routine work. But today I've got a few cycling puzzles to figure out. But what do you want? What brings you here?"

He looked at his watch. "Don't you have a meeting? Here, let me take off this dirty apron and we can talk."

"I don't care about the grease, Tony. Just hold me, hon. I really need you to. Les was murdered. Krypto was killed. It's like it didn't happen. Nobody on campus seems real. Amend that. No faculty seems real. Amend again. None of the guys in the English department seem real. Some of the priorities and attitudes they're displaying have gone beyond heartless to just plain crass. I need a heavy dose of your reality, Tony, grease and all."

"Oh, poor Mary Babe. Here's a hug, but only a quickie hug. Sorry I can't oblige you with some reality right now. I have to work, and too many people are around. Later tonight . . . ."

We actually did make plans then for dinner at Our Place with a codicil, the evening to be continued . . . .

Who would have dreamt that a bike shop would now be my safe house!

Chapter Six

"The first myth of management is that it exists."

Robert Heller, 1972

❧

I was afraid of being late, so after receiving that much needed hug, I half-jogged back to campus. As I passed the Buckeye, I wondered if I hadn't been happier, certainly less stressed when my office was there. During those first weeks, I did get a kind of admiration from my students by requiring meetings with the message, "MAKE (appointments at) BIG BUCKS." But I knew that I was better off politically and logistically in Loomis Hall. And Les's and Krypto's murders would have affected me no matter where I was officed.

By the time I got back to campus and was close enough to the Lounge to smell the Starbucks, everyone else was there. I could hear the uneven buzz of conversation, stimulated by the murder, mixed with Roger Christian's regular whining, stimulated by his need for attention. The tone was different from the usual ferocity of one-upmanship that dominated our meetings and made each contender try to top last week's 'casual' criticism of "Baudelaire's socio-economic cannibalism" or "the whole hierarchy of meanings that can be constructed from the hieroglyphics on the white whale," or anything higher on the ladder of critical abstraction.

I knew I was late so I tried to unobtrusively sneak in. Impossible. I felt that I bumped into and tripped over everything and everyone. Really, I just tripped over Roger's ceaselessly swinging foot, and that sort of propelled me into the back of Charlie Volstadt's chair. Was Roger developing a nervous twitch or was I looking for an excuse for my clumsiness? Or a clue about Les's murderer? I looked again. Roger caught my eye and tried to furtively clasp his hands around the offending knee.

Gary, who as presiding officer 'owns' the power chair at the front of the room, waited until all four heads already there turned to watch me stumble in. He had his audience and deliberately addressed me, timing his remarks for his collegial sycophants. "Welcome, Ms. Goldberg. By the way, I always meant to ask you if you were related to Whoopi." This was followed by much laughter from other members of the department, led by Roger (laughing loudly is almost as good as whining as an attention-getting mechanism). God, was I embarrassed. I knew that some of the laughter was forced, but that didn't keep me from feeling like a goofus. Gary asks me questions like that at every single possible academic function, and I can never come back with a politically correct answer.

"Just six degrees of separation," I answered, forcing a smile only made possible by envisioning that corkscrew stuck into Gary, which started me on an interesting train of thought. I spent much of the rest of the meeting following it, wondering if Gary could be, in fact, the murderer. Why not? He was the only one with a cruel streak. It showed through in little, mean actions and somehow in his physicality. He isn't big exactly. In fact, he has an average build. But he seems big. He seems threatening.

I remembered at the beginning of the semester when I was so pleased with myself because I had rooted a rather interesting variation of wandering Jew from the one that still blooms on my desk. I had enough to pot a plant for each member of the department as an office-warming gift. It was meant as a metaphor for me as a scholar who had worked at a number of places and was now ready to settle down. It was the kind of personal metaphor I knew my colleagues would understand and appreciate. All except Gary. Gary not only wouldn't accept my gift, but he also stood in the corridor and yelled at me never ever to even think about giving him a plant. I could have died. It wasn't a Venus's flytrap, for goodness sakes. If he didn't want it, he could have just taken it and thrown it away instead of making such a scene that people came out of their offices to see what was going on. Well, that doesn't exactly make Gary a murderer, I argued back at me, but I can't think of any one else who is as power driven or as nasty. And the murder did happen in his office.

While I was pondering the pleasant possibility of someone I disliked being guilty, Gary called the meeting to order. "Even though we are all affected by this unpleasantness," he intoned, "we'll follow the agenda as planned with the addition, of course, of my suggestions for our public reaction to Les's untimely, and I might add, unseemly, death."

Squirming with disbelief (we were going to accuse Les of bad taste in being murdered?), I almost missed Stew's thoughtful interruption, "I know we don't start our meetings with prayers and I know that some people here are actively against prayers of any kind, but it seems to me that we should have a moment of silent meditation or maybe a verse. Unfortunately, all I can think of right now is:

> *How pleasant to know Mr. Lear*
> *Who has written such volumes of stuff*
> *Some think him ill-tempered and queer,*
> *But a few think him pleasant enough . . . .*

Straightening his off-the-rack tweed jacket, he quickly went on, not allowing any interruptions. "We could alter it," he said and soberly read:

> *How pleasant to know Mr. Les*
> *Who has written such volumes of stuff*
> *Some think him too allergic, a mess,*
> *But a few think him pleasant enough . . . .*

The awkward silence that greeted this attempt at humor made me realize that I wasn't the only one wriggling with embarrassment. Maybe, I wondered, could the murderer be Stew? He thinks of himself, and often is, the wit. Sometimes there's only a thin line between funny and sick. I tried to look interested in what was being said, but really I was trying to figure out if there was a joke, a sick, sick joke connecting Stew to this murder. If there was, I wasn't getting it.

My façade of attentiveness was shattered when never-spontaneous Charlie Volstadt reacted to those awful limericks by actually jumping up. I was so startled that I almost did too. "Stop it, Stew," he ordered. "You might be the department's joker-in-chief, but come on, that's a little out of place. How about the few lines from a requiem that I read at Rotary yesterday in memory of our past president? As Joseph Conrad might have said, 'Les was one of us,' you know, a member of the department even if he was only with us for a short time." He pulled a small card from his wallet and straightening his tweed jacket, a noticeably better cut than Stew's, read,

> But open converse is there none
> So much the vital spirits sink
> To see the vacant chair, and think,
> "How good! How kind! And he is gone."

Charlie concluded with a smile—at me. Was this his idea of flirting? I couldn't force my mouth into a return smile. Instead, I felt I literally gaped, open-mouthed at him.

Then Gary, ostentatiously straightening his imported tweed jacket to make us fully conscious that it was better cut, finer wool, and the only bespoke jacket at the meeting, put a stop to the competitive versifying with, "Enough. The most noticeable thing Les ever did in his life was to get killed. What's there to talk about? We'll just tell Vice President Mossberg that we had a private memorial service. And your reading from Tennyson's In Memoriam, Charlie, was it! Now to the point, who will teach Les's two sections?" That made me stop thinking about the possibility of Gary's or Stew's involvement with the murder long enough to wonder if there were any boundaries to the egocentricities of members of this department. Was it my imagination or was everyone getting weirder?

To be fair, some genuine emotion was displayed. Krypto was quietly discussed with affection, and in a low voice Roger said that he had just seen a bumper sticker that said, "My Border Collie Is Smarter Than Your Honor Student." We nodded agreement, while Stew was so vehement he forgot about the on-going meeting and pounded on his chair's arm: "I knew it. I knew it." A whispered side bar analyzing Krypto's I.Q. followed until Gary noticed we weren't paying attention to his every word. With that realization came immediate and complicated diagrams of schedule changes on the chalkboard.

Against the background of that necessary rescheduling and the resulting whining, I continued to figure things out, keeping what I hope was an interested face. Each of us was a suspect. I know that I didn't do it. I know that Tony didn't do it either. The thought of Tony caused a brief mentally wandering: Is it true that men think more about sex than women do? Am I odd? I know when I think of Tony, I do not think about the book he's writing.

I pulled myself back to thoughts of the murderer. I had four in-house possibilities, when last seen all trying to outdo each other in displaying their professorial tweeds. Why couldn't the criminal be seemingly dull, old Rotary-minded Charlie? That very proper bank president façade of his is just a façade. Or as Gary sneered at him-when it was his turn to be sneered at-"I see through you and your well-schooled dichotomies." Students told me early on that Charlie tries so hard to be one of them that during freshman orientation-Oops, I'd better get it right even when I'm just thinking-during "new student" orientation week, he went back to the dorm with his new advisees and tried to roll a joint with them, much to their embarrassment.

I suddenly put my detecting skills to a practical use and concluded that in the middle of my daydream and plotting, the meeting must have been adjourned. At least everyone else was getting up and leaving, so only slightly red in the face and only dropping two books, I did too.

"Wait, Mary Beth. I want to tell you something," Roger called and walked out with me, making things worse by trying to straighten my not-quite-falling-again books. "Mary Beth, I wanted you to know that everyone in administration is talking about how popular your E.M. Forster course is. They say it's the hottest class in the English department, and this was before you became a college celebrity by finding, well, almost finding Les's body. You know how numbers count with the deans. I think you're going to make the English department cost effective all by yourself."

"Uh, thank you, uh, Roger," I mumbled with my usual grace in accepting a compliment. What I was thinking as I mumbled was, is he trying to deflect suspicion by getting on the good side of me? I immediately chastised myself for not being able to accept a bid toward collegiality. After all, if a class titled, "The Forbidden Lust of E.M. Forster" wasn't going to attract non-majors as well as majors, what would?

Chapter Seven

*"... spread abroad a spirit of general suspicion and
distrust, which accepts rumor and gossip in place of
undismayed and unintimidated inquiry."*

*Judge Learned Hand, speech to the Board of Regents,
University of the State of New York, 1952*

❧

I hurried away from Roger and the aftermath of the
meeting toward my refuge, Tony. It was either Tony or that
post-traumatic-stress counseling that Vice President
Mossberg had offered me at the Student Wellness Center.
The Wellness Center is the result of the think-positive
modernization that reigned on campus a few years ago. It
is the new label put on the old building that formerly
housed the Student Health Care Clinic.

Mossberg, herself, is nice. You could see that she had
been a keen, maybe peachy, young woman with a keen,
maybe peachy, hair-do twenty years ago, and she had seen

no reason to change it. Could I say anything to her about still keeping that hair-do? No, Mary Beth!

All campus news reaches my friend, Janet Purlis, Curly Curt's wife. That night many phone calls and emails helped transmit some of her newly acquired news to me. I learned through Jan, one of the two pillars of my private girlfriend-grapevine, that maybe I should have hung around a few minutes after the meeting. Maybe I would have picked-up some information. Maybe I would have become more integrated with my peers. And just maybe I should stop thinking in triplicate possibilities.

What I heard later was that when I left, the *aprés* meeting began in earnest. My source: Janet. Janet's source: Curt. Janet is a jewelry maker and is detail oriented. She is also an excellent listener. My imagination helped to fill in the few blanks Janet left, but there weren't many.

She reported that the *après* chat started with Roger's turning to Charlie and Stew with the suggestion of some follow-up coffee and conversation. Gary had already fled. Even though the department is his playpen, he often separates himself from his would-be cronies physically by space and psychologically by intimating he has more important things to do. The three good-old-boys of the English dept. turned back into the lounge, all directed toward the English corner, delineated from the rest of the lounge area by the requisite faded Persian rug.

I'd been there enough times. I could easily visualize the scene. The four worn brown leather arm chairs, the scarred mahogany bookcases filled with well-bound classics, and the rather dim lighting due to the pseudo vellum lamp shades, all arranged in the far corner, are their refuge as Tony is mine. The old club shabbiness of the corner was the inspiration of the interior designer who had done what he could to make his Midfield employers realize their dream-world of teaching at Oxbridge. The rigidly posed photographs of Midfield's benign past presidents in ornate, imitation gold frames don't quite take the place of portraits of royal ancestors and benefactors, but it had been worth a try.

As the three went directly to their rightful chairs, they greeted Janet's husband Curt Perlis, the fourth musketeer, the buddy who was the most powerful net player at their once a week doubles game. Curt had been grading papers while he waited for their regular meeting to be over. I didn't mention to Janet when she was telling me this, but the students call Curt "Curley Purley." They've got it just right. Curt has tightly curled blond hair that he wears short, close to the head, and a pearly white, toothy smile. That smile is most evident when he is playing mentor, as he repeatedly does, to minority students. The problem for the students he mentors is that he is fickle. He has been a consistent and good friend to Tony and me, but he habitually stops mentoring one minority student if another more controversial and, therefore, more interesting, student comes along. I wonder if he could have been in the process of dropping Les and his thesis on colonialism. Maybe he wanted to be a paternal figure for someone working on a trendier project. Maybe he was just plain bored with Les and all of his problems, from allergic to academic. Les certainly had the knack of using his complaints to dull down otherwise interesting conversations. But he wouldn't have had to kill Les to keep from yawning.

As Janet described it, Roger was the one who got the conversational ball rolling.

"Tea is necessary for thinking." Roger prescribed and poured. "Anyway, that nerdy boyfriend of Mary Beth's told me once that someone, was it Fielding? Was it Congreve? Not important, someone said, 'love and scandal are the best sweeteners of tea.'"

"No thanks," Curt said, illustrating his personal choice by holding up a thermos and a coffee mug.

Charlie took a flask out of his briefcase, explaining, "I've got a better sweetener, better than scandal, anyway." He passed it around, adding, "This is the closest we're going to get to a genuine hot rum toddy at this club. Pity. There's nothing like one on a cool October day-or any other day, for that matter."

Roger went on as if Charlie hadn't spoken, but not forgetting to help himself to some rum, "Now that I've said it, Tony is slightly odd isn't he? Do you think he did it?"

"You mean murdered Les? I don't think he's so odd. I've met plenty of these super logical engineer-types before."

"Who work in a bike shop?" Stew threw in, stirring his tea for emphasis. "And who caresses his girlfriend with words? It's 'Mary Babe this' and 'Mary Best that.'"

Roger ignored him as well and answered Charlie's earlier question. "Yes, he could have murdered Les and Krypto, too. Of course that's also odd. Why in the world would anyone have murdered Krypto? Say, how did she get that name anyway? From some Superman fan on campus?"

"No, it has a slightly more intellectual origin," said Stew. Charlie growled, "The bitch just showed up on campus one day. No one knew anything about her background, so a Greek student called her 'Krypto' for 'hidden' or 'secret,' and it stuck."

Roger cut in, "Excuse me, gentlemen. Could we get back to the murders, please? Say, has anyone talked with Abby McKenzie?"

Curt answered (I'll bet his tone of voice announced his perceived scientific superiority to McKenzie). "Who do you mean? Abby J. McKenzie, the school doctor? Or the A. J. McKenzie who moonlights as the Medical Examiner?"

Roger laughed, "Neither. The McKenzie who saw to it that Krypto's shots were up to date and that she had something to eat besides the pizza the kids gave her each day."

Curt put in, "You want to talk with Krypto's doctor? You think Krypto confided in her doctor about her enemies. Come on . . . "

"Krypto was pretty smart," Stew said, pushing himself into the conversation again. "All Border collies are. I've heard them called 'the wisest dog in the world.' There's even an Internet Border Collie Museum. I kid you not. The museum has permanent and changing exhibits just like a real museum."

Janet was so proud and pleased to tell me that it was her Curt then who came to the defense of my Tony.

He took over the conversation, "I doubt if any one of us really thinks the murderer is Tony. I would take any suspicions about him with a grain of sodium chloride. But we know it has to be someone with access to Loomis Hall. And who is that? The janitorial staff's big gripe is that they have to go over to Administration each day to pick up keys. Now that irritation is working in their favor. There's no record of anyone picking up the keys."

"That would have been a dead give away," Stew interjected with a self-conscious smile.

Curt stared him down, " . . . plus Vice President Mossberg has looked into the situation and acquitted them. Anyway, they always clean first thing in the morning. That leaves you three guys, or Gary, or that infamous team of Mary Beth and Tony. I know Mary Beth and Tony. Believe me, they are not Bonnie and Clyde. They are good people. But why?" he persevered. "Why such a limited pool of suspects?"

"Elementary, my dear Watsons," Charlie answered, addressing the group. "Gary locked our corridor when he left early Monday afternoon. We members of the English department are the only ones with keys." Charlie settled back into his chair, tented his thick fingers, and waited.

Janet chuckled when she told me this next part. Curt really threw a spanner in the works when he said, "Sorry, Charlie. If you're basing suspicion on corridor access, you could consider me a suspect, too."

Curt got their full attention with that remark.

"Yes. I've got a key. The 'key society' isn't quite as exclusive as you thought."

"But how?" "When?" Different voices using different words asked the same question.

"Les gave it to me," Curt answered. "He was my protégé and wanted to make it easy for me to come to his office."

"But Les didn't have a key. He was a part-timer. He wasn't supposed to have a key," Charlie cried.

Silence. I could just see each professor giving a quick suspicious look around, followed by each person's eyes settling non-confrontationally on his own shoe tops, waiting.

Roger stiffened. "I'm the culprit here," he announced. "He cajoled me. Les wanted his own key and I thought 'why not'? I had a copy made of mine."

"Who gave whom the key is a moot point," he continued. "Les obviously wasn't the murderer. I wasn't. But I'm sure the culprit was someone on campus. Look, Midfield is not exactly a 24-hour town. It's interesting that Les and Krypto were killed during school hours in what is supposed to be a locked corridor. Sure sounds to me as if someone is on a school schedule with access to English department scheduling and keys. How did Tony get into the offices anyway? "

Roger turned and addressed Curt, contradicting his earlier Tony-theory, "How Tony got in isn't important. You know better than anyone that Mary Beth and Tony wouldn't have touched Krypto. You're the one who told me that they thought she was a member of their family, the baby they haven't had-yet! Anyone could see that Krypto thought they were splendid."

Ever the scientist, Curt interjected, "Has anyone contacted the Ohio State Veterinarian College?"

"Oh, sure, they've got sleuths there on staff," Stew chuckled with delight. "They must have a special course 'Canine Killers or Dogs I Have Murdered.'"

"Or wish I had," Charlie muttered.

"Come on, guys. We wouldn't have any trouble figuring out who the perpetrator is if we could figure out any motivation. Go back to my question," Roger insisted, "or my implied question. Forget the Krypto part. Obviously, it's Les's murder that is important. Has anyone thought that one of us could be next. I want to find that killer. Any suggestions? Any suggestion would be better than those silver S.O.S. whistles they're handing out. Where did our dear president get that idea?"

"I didn't know Les very well," Charlie continued, "but as far as I could see, all he was interested in was finishing his dissertation and being with that delicious girlfriend of his, M & M, um umm. That would be some trick or treat."

"And a job," Roger threw in, speaking so strongly that he shook his tea from the cup to the saucer to his khakis. "He was desperate for a job. I know he was desperate."

Stew was talking at the same time, "Charlie, you've had enough 'trick or treat' problems around here when it wasn't even autumn. Let's stick to the subject. And that's Les-who seemed pretty happy to me. But remember the old Midfield saying, 'He who gets too big for his britches will be exposed in the end.'"

"I'm trying to ignore you and your old Midfield sayings," Curt added. "I can't see any motivation and I think I know Les better than anyone in his own department. I still have some of his books in my office, books he left Monday morning and was going to pick up later. How sad that there is no 'later' for him."

"What books?" Stew's interest was piqued.

"Nothing to get emotional about. He had some of his usual anti-colonialism books, old and new. I remember one of the newer ones because I read it and liked it myself. I go for that superficially plain, Kafkaesque style. It's *Waiting for the Barbarians* by J. M. Coetzee, the South African. The others were the kind of academic stuff you guys are always writing or reading, some inter-library loans by Frantz Fanon. One article was something like 'Ahab and Paternalism.' Another, 'Colonial Imagining, Race and Authority in . . . ' someone. Not my field. I can get the titles if they're important."

"I don't suppose there were any of my articles?" Stew inquired. "You know, Les's academic interests and mine ran on parallel tracts. Ho, ho, guys, little polemic joke there."

"I'll look to see if Les left any notes in the books that could be meaningful," Curt offered, "Then I'll return them to the Buckeye Library for him."

Stew inserted, "Passing the Buck, Curt?" and, realizing

the inappropriateness of his remark, added, "Sorry. A jokette. I couldn't help it."

Curt was serious: "It's the least I can do. Funny, I feel that by returning the books I'll be making a little pilgrimage in memory of Les. All of his plans: dissertation, job, Marguerita-they're all ruined aren't they? Permanently."

That remark quieted almost everyone for a minute. Charlie even stopped stirring his tea, but in a few seconds, went on talking, "Les's notes bring up a potentially inciteful question. Stew, you're familiar with his dissertation. Are there any clues in it? Anything he was writing about that we should be aware of?"

"No, no. Not at all. His Thesis Interruptis is a result, not a cause. Les is another example of a potentially decent writer ruined by grad school. His dissertation started out with some originality, but developed into a pretty pedestrian examination of 'Black vs. White in Melville and Poe.' No calls for revolution or anything like that."

Curt leaned forward, "Come on, Stew, it couldn't be pedestrian if it's grounded in your wonderful work. What was that impossible title of yours? Something that sounds like linguistics, but turns out to be a post-colonialism study? I remember, 'The Raj Response to Comparative Grammars of the Modern Aryan Languages.' Love it."

Charlie called quits on one of the English faculty's favorite pastimes, teasing Stew, "O.K., we've got this nice kid, and I might add, our department's only African American lecturer, dead. We don't have any idea about why he was killed. We don't have a clue as to who did it. Where do we go from here? For a first step, I'll pass the flask again."And he did.

Charlie talked as he topped-off cups of tea and Curt's coffee. "I know I've got a little reputation for drinking and, you know what? I like it. It makes me a kind of mini-celebrity with the kids on campus. I try to spread the word that I like to cook with wine, too. Sometimes I even put it in the food," he added, grinning at what he considered his devilish humor.

Stew acknowledged Charlie's wisecrack with the slightest of smiles and returned to topic A. "I suppose the next step is someone's asking for alibis," Stew contributed. "And I have mine. I was home. Sally was there, too. But probably they won't count a spouse's alibi. I would be all set with Sally as witness and I know you were out of town, Curt. That leaves you two, Roger and Charlie."

"In my office." "At home," came the two over-lapping replies.

"Well," Roger said, "I guess Officer Yoder will look into all of our alibis. I'll need another one if I do what I feel like when that guy says, 'just call me Seth' one more time. Or maybe I'll use some of my choice Shakespearean epithets."

"I know that folksiness bothers you, Roger," Stew almost sneered, "but we still should play fair with him. Seth is the detective on this case, and, as far as I know, not one of us has told him about the fight."

Curt put his coffee mug on the table and leaned forward,

"I wasn't there, and it's probably not important to the investigation, but you're right, Stew. One of you who was at that meeting should discuss it with Seth."

"I suggested it, but I'm not going to do it," Stew said defiantly. "I have a more comedic turn of mind than 'Just Call Me Strait-Laced' does. I'd never be able to seriously describe Les and Gary getting down and dirty to him. Hiring is inevitably contentious, but in the English department it's getting to be more than a tad ridiculous. Roger and Charlie, it's up to you."

Roger and Charlie looked at each other and shrugged acquiescence. Charlie spoke for both of them, "It's a minor point. But you're correct. Officer Yoder should know. We'll take care of it right now."

Janet and I knew these four guys so well, we could even figure out their inflections and body language.

Then, Jan said, Roger, who more or less had called the meeting, more or less ended it with a typical do-nothing decision, unanimously approved, "For now, let's leave the solution to Les's murder up to the proper authorities. If they don't make some visible progress by a week from today, let's meet again, form an action committee."

Stew interrupted, "Action committee? Who's the first to see an oxymoron here?"

Roger remained undeterred: "Action committee of the whole, elect an appropriate (ahem!) chairman, apportion the workload to two subcommittees, and possibly propose some investigative direction."

"Excellent." "Kudos, old boy." "And a Right ho! from me."

If I hadn't run off to find Tony, if I had stayed on for the *après* chat, what could I have added? A hearty pip, pip?

Chapter Eight

"The Incidence of Crime on the Campuses of U.S.
Postsecondary Education Institutions" at

<www.ed.gov/offices/OPE/PPI/ReportToCongress.pdf>

৯৯

Detective Seth Yoder often hummed to himself and talked to himself (so his subordinates whispered). And he was proud of the comprehensive longhand notes he wrote to himself as preliminary and personal reports on all Midfield crimes under his jurisdiction. He wrote his own impressions, as many good police officers do, for himself, not for his file. He found that these notes helped him to remember details, organize his thoughts, and write up the top-notch final reports he would eventually send to the Mayor of Midfield or the President of the College, depending on crime and locale. This time with a murder on his hands, he was more precise than usual as he began his personal file. He wanted a name, a catchy title, for the crime or the criminal. People remembered "The Railway Murders" or "The Boston Strangler," and Midfield Campus College's murder could make national news. The possibility was strong that President Bender under the Clery Act revisions of 1998 (requiring college crime statistics to be reported) would do more than the minimum. Once the case was solved, he might send Midfield, Ohio's, Detective Seth Yoder's final, full report to the United State Department of Education.

Permitting himself a brief vision of a national reputation, just the reputation-Seth wouldn't want to live or work anyplace but in Midfield-he unconsciously licked his finger and turned to his untitled page one where he carefully lettered in Midfield Murders. After a few seconds of thought, he added a second title line "referred to by the press as The McMurders" and started to reread his notes. A persistent knocking caused him to break off in the middle of this critical work. He looked up with irritation to hear Miller announce, "Two suspects to see you, Sheriff."

Seth made a quick mental note to chastise Miller for his lack of professionalism: two 'suspects,' indeed!

The confidential word I had from Janet was that Charlie and Roger had left the group of four and, as they promised, made straight for Seth's office. On the way, they had chatted about presentation and strategy.

"How far back should we go?" Roger asked. "Didn't Les and Gary have a history of ill-will before the fight?"

"That's right," Charlie replied. "You're not teaching this

term, so you wouldn't have been at the meeting regarding final class schedules. You missed Gary's magnanimous gesture, his offer to teach one section of the lowest of the low, First Year Comp."

"Yes. I heard about it. In fact Les told me. We were exchanging gripes about Gary. You know how much Gary wants to keep me from voting in the department. Les and I were having a regular Gary Hake Appreciation Association meeting! I guess when Gary offered to teach Comp., he wanted the rest of you to know that he feels your pain."

"His section and Les's were offered at the same time," Charlie hurried to keep up with Roger and resumed his narration. "Somehow word had gotten out to incoming students regarding who was the better teacher. Fifteen students signed up for Les's class, six for Gary's. You know the result. Les's section was cancelled, reducing his work load to two classes, not enough to live on if it hadn't been for Margarita's job. All students were reassigned to Gary's section."

"We always come up with reasons to off Gary, not the other way around. Well, it's not pertinent and here we are at the Court House," Roger pointed. "You do the talking; you can just call him Seth."

Roger and Charlie entered the building and turned toward Seth's office. The door was never locked. "It belongs to the people," was Seth's explanation. As Miller announced the two men, they entered with the pompous assurance they felt suitable for dealings with 'their' public servant. Without waiting for his invitations, both men pulled up chairs and made themselves comfortable in the small quarters. This was easier for Roger with his slight build than it was for Charlie who overlapped the wooden slatted chair he uncomfortably shifted around in. Uncomfortably or guiltily? Seth wondered as he studied his visitors.

Polite greetings were exchanged. Remarks were made about the weather. Then silence.

Roger stiffened and stepped into the void. "Charlie will speak for both of us because he was there."

"Where?" Seth asked.

"Oh, yeah, he was there at the department meeting. Anyway, Charlie will speak, and I'll fill in anything he leaves out. Go ahead, Charlie."

"Well, Seth," Charlie started, "no one likes to be a tale bearer. Do you say tattle tale?"

Seth looked at him. "I speak the same English you do, Charlie. You're saying that you don't like to inform on someone?"

"That's right. But Curley, that is, Curt Perlis and Stew Jones decided that the two of us-Roger and I-should try to explain to you . . . "

"Get to the point, Charlie. It's late in the day and I still have work to do."

No more preambles. Charlie got to the point. "At our meeting about a month ago, the first regular Monday department meeting in October, Gary Hake asked for a volunteer to go with him to the Modern Language Association meeting in New York over Christmas break. You should know, Seth, that we've been criticized by the Accreditation Committee and our own vice president because our hiring process is slow and late. Interviews were being conducted in March, long after the very best candidates had received offers. They complained that the department has not been in competition for the most outstanding younger prospects in years.

"So Gary wanted someone to work with him on interviewing applicants for an opening that was coming up. No one wanted to go. Christmas break, we call it 'Mid-winter Break' now," Charlie stopped to explain his political correctness. "Mid-winter isn't religious unless you belong to some pagan cult, and the break is a time to be off campus, to be with our families, to re-charge our batteries, and, in Les's case, to finish his dissertation.

"But Les had a conflict. More than he wanted time with Margarita," Roger continued Charlie's narration. "And more than he wanted time to work on his dissertation, Les wanted to get on the good side of Gary because he eventually wanted to teach full-time in Midfield's English department. So he volunteered. Gary told him that appointments had been made with ten excellent candidates and that the two of them would do team interviewing."

Charlie picked up the tale, "You could see that Les thought he had racked up some big brownie points. Roger has been on his side right along, and I think that Stew has, too. Now he had Gary. Just as the meeting ended, someone got to Les and explained what was really going on. The new position being created would combine Les's part-time Composition sections with the full-time work load Les was aspiring to. In other words, he was being used to interview candidates for a new job, composed of his own job that he would be kicked out of plus the Assistant Professorship he had thought he was in line for."

"Les was livid," Roger explained. "And who could blame him. He had been the victim of a very dirty trick. Worse, he had been publicly victimized in front of his peers. Before Gary could leave the room, Les was on top of him. I give Gary physical credit for not running away; he is a tad older than Les. The two of them had a real knock down, dragged out, fist fight before we could separate them.

"A fist fight between gentlemen in the English literature department of Midfield Campus College was unprecedented, really unimaginable except that we had all just seen it happen. No one has referred to it since that afternoon, but we thought you should know, Seth." Roger ahemmed a bit, "Also, Seth, all of us would appreciate it if you would not tell Gary where you got this information. Let him think it is general campus talk."

"Thank you, gentlemen. The incident you have reported is quite interesting," Seth said. "I'll get back to you later with specific questions asking for more details. Meanwhile, don't worry. I won't mention this visit to Gary. Those of us in detective work always protect our sources."

After Charlie and Roger left, Seth licked his finger again as he leafed through pages and returned thoughtfully to the careful study of his **McMurder** notes:

> 1. Victim(s): Lester Delaney, age 28, male, African American, finishing dissertation, ABD, (all but dissertation), teaching part-time at the college. Any other source of income?

Here he added:

> Quick tempered? Public fist fight with Gary Hake? All questioned say no racial motivation, but . . .
> Krypto, age $4\,^1/_2$, female, Border collie. Seemed in good health. Shots up to date.
> 2. Date: ME places both murders sometime Monday mid-afternoon, one to two hours prior to English department regular weekly 5:00 o'clock meeting. Initial report based on body and room temperatures. Final reports due.
> 3. Place: Midfield Campus College, Midfield, Ohio, Loomis Hall, department of English, office of Chair of English department, Dr. Gary H. Hake.
> 4. Location of bodies: Both bodies found on floor of office, Delaney prone.
> 5. Cause of deaths: Delaney unknown, pending autopsy. Hit by paperweight, but amount of blood makes this a highly unlikely cause of death, though President Fairchild Bender already announced contusion as cause of death. Some swelling of face. Result of blow?

Dog (Krypto) presumably by corkscrew found in throat, pending autopsy.

6. Motivation: both unknowns

7. Body discovered by: Dr. Anthony (Tony) Bartlett, engineer now employed by Bob's Superbikes, writing book, fiancee of MB Goldberg and alibied by her (!) How did he get in locked corridor?

2nd person on scene: Dr. Mary Beth Goldberg, Visiting Professor at the College, English Dept., teaches English lit (Forster) and utopian lit. Author of some books, well respected in fields. Alibied by Bartlett (!)

8. Possible scenarios:

Delaney killed dog?

Bartlett killed Delaney and dog, then gets Goldberg to 'discover' bodies.

Bartlett and Goldberg commit murders together.

Most likely-unknown subject kills Delaney and dog.

Question! Which victim did unsub kill first?

9. Other possible suspects: Margarita Maria Berenguer, girl friend of Delaney, some connection to college as teaches one section Spanish. from El Salvador, check if U.S. citizen.

Dr. Gary Hake, Chair of Eng. Dept., teaches American lit, esp. puritans and Mark Twain. Very verbal. Had to cut off his explanation of academic hierarchy. Wanted me to understand that he's at the top.

Seth expanded his earlier notes to add his new information:

> Public fist fight with vic one month ago over departmental politics, specifically hiring and firing (hiring new prof to take Les's place).
>
> Dr. W. Stewart Jones, teaches colonialism, whatever that means, and all early lit-(Beowulf, Canterbury Tales, The Tale of Genji). Said, "speaking of death, did you ever hear the one about the rabbi, the priest and the minister when they got to St. Peter?" I cut him off too. A nervous reaction? Why? What's with these guys?
>
> Dr. Charles Volstadt, teaches contemporary British and Amer. lit, literary criticism. Seems more normal, though smarmy-nervous and upset. If reports of Eng. Dept. meeting are correct, why was he prepared with memorial poem? Check if Rotary excuse is true.
>
> Dr. Roger Christian, temporarily on loan to admin-istration, community relations dept., and (he importantly tells me) writing a history of the college, teaches Brit. lit., from Shakespeare to Bloomsbury, also nervous and upset. More tense than anyone. He was seated across the desk from me (all were). In Christian's case, could feel regular vibrations of leg shaking through desktop.

> Dr. Curt Perlis, chem. Prof., (poisons?) but real
> interest is hematology. Sometime mentor to
> Delaney. Angry with me because couldn't have
> blood sample and no wine for him to test.
> Called Curly Purley, affectionately or not?
> These people seem to identify themselves by their class
> subjects. What does this mean if anything? Is what
> they do, who they are?

Seth stopped writing, hummed a little, and (according to Amos) said out loud, "I never before thought that knowing there are more murderers than college professors in the U.S. would make me happy, but, somehow, today it does." He went back to his report.

> 10. Evidence (so far)
> Paperweight. All identify it as Gary's. Fingerprints?
> Waiting for evidence analysis report.
> Corkscrew. Belongs to Gary? If not, who? Ordinary
> wine shop corkscrew? Suspects MB, Hake, Jones,
> and Christian all say something like, "I think I have
> one like that." Fingerprints? Blood samples?
> Awaiting evidence analysis report from B.C.I.
> Cork found in wastebasket. Related to finding
> corkscrew or not? Corks in wastebaskets not
> unusual. Wine always served at faculty parties,
> often at informal meetings. Prints? Awaiting evidence
> report here too. Some smudged brand markings.
> Red stain on cork is wine. Smells like normal red

wine to me. Check out four cork questions. But where's the bottle? And glass or glasses?

Seth picked up a bright blue felt pen and added in caps:

NEED: Cause, official time of death

NEED: Alibis for department members and Perlis and Berenguer

NEED: Motivation. Sex? Money? Power? There doesn't seem to be much of any of the basic motivators around here

NEED: to be certain that Les was intended victim

Check with ME re blood on paperweight, autopsy, etc. Check on Wednesday, McKenzie available. Her day off at the College.

Possibility of DNA testing?

Have called in State help: the Bureau of Criminal Investigation.

Outside of Seth's office, Midfield's business and commercial day was winding down. Seth found he was too. But he took time to open a new computer file, label it "Midfield Murders," and enter an abbreviated and depersonalized form of the impressions he had noted. After painstakingly using spell-check, he put the full original notes of the case in his private file (top shirt pocket), and left for the day, mulling motive, means, and opportunity.

Chapter Nine

*"There is nothing which has yet been contrived by man
by which so much happiness is produced as by a good
tavern or inn."*

Samuel Johnson, from Boswell, Life of Johnson, March
21, 1776

ॐ

Tony looked great as usual with his ponytail slightly
askew, but with his pens neatly aligned in his pocket
protector. He was checking out the latest product reviews
in this month's Bicycling Magazine while waiting for me at
our regular after-the-department-meeting refuge. I always
left those Monday evening meetings, including tonight's
Tuesday alternative, too emotionally high or low to cook.
But I was never so ecstatic or depressed that I could eat
Tony's culinary inventions. He could prepare entire meals on
one hot plate and the souped-up radiator in his apartment.
He was already planning his next book, *No-Kitchen
Cuisine: Radiator Recipes.*

Our Place is charming. At least that's what Tony and I thought when we went there the first time, the second time, third, and fourth too. By our fifth visit, we realized that Our Place represented 50% of the non-fast food restaurants in Midfield. We still admired the candles in old Chianti bottles, the checked tablecloths, the almost clean aprons on the rotating crew of student waiters. By now we had settled in, not seeing, just feeling happy to have someone else cook and wash dishes one night a week. With our decision that *su cocina es mi cocina*, we had stopped consulting the menu and trustingly ordered the special without even asking about it.

But we were always careful to sit in chairs that faced northwest to benefit from productive energy. Our pal Su Ming, local entrepreneur and feng shui practitioner, had rearranged the chairs for us one night, explaining that this new geographic alignment would insure our flow of chi. Tuesday night I felt I was in such a precarious emotional position that I could use every bit of extra energy and 'harmonious order' I could get.

"Hey, Gus," Tony, who was already seated, greeted our favorite waiter, "bring in the bottled lightning, a clean tumbler, and a corkscrew."

"You can't catch me, Tony," I heard Gus replying as I suavely approached our table. "That's from *Nicholas Nickleby*. I took a Dickens course last semester. I know." Gus was already carrying over a carafe of our own favorite bottled lightning, Valpolicella, as he answered Tony. In my deft maneuvering past other diners, I managed to drop only three of the books I was carrying. Fortunately they were paperbacks so I could scoop them all up in one smooth bend. "Neat new jeans, Tony," I noticed as I joined him. This must have been the millionth time I thought how terrific Tony looks in black jeans and a black shirt, even though his ponytail could use the male equivalent of a scrunchie. Strangely enough, he doesn't mind hearing about how good he looks. He knows his all black, mad scientist look is well-constructed and likes it to be appreciated. Once he returned a green sweater I had given him for a present, saying. "I'm a city person, Mary Best. Green is not my favorite color."

He smiled a greeting in response to mine and brushed his hair away from his face. Tony's pony tail certainly isn't a compensatory one like the ones sported by some of the older Profs who look completely bald if first seen from the front. Tony was happy, as usual, to have me continue to chat about him and my Our Place observations. While talking, I unfolded my napkin, then took a few minutes to study the other diners instead of him. Was the murderer here? Was he staking out his next victim? Was I getting paranoid?

Sipping that first welcome glass of red wine, maybe it was the first two glasses, we quickly passed over the highs and lows of the day and got to what was really on our minds. For once it wasn't us and our relationship and where it was going and where we were going. Though I noticed that even through my frantic narrative of the day's events, Tony still kept one section of his mind open for his

Bartlett's Better Quotations. He had certainly whipped out his pen in a hurry when I came to the part about Stew's and Charlie's "memorial" readings.

"Look, Mary Beth," Tony said pushing aside the candle and its twinned bottle holding a lone white lily. How apropos, I thought, noticing the flower, What did Our Place do? Rob a cemetery? Tony was continuing, "It has to be someone in your department who killed Krypto and Les, that is, if they were killed at the same time. The police can tell us that."

"Why does it have to be someone from the English department, Tony?" I asked. "There are plenty of other creeps in other departments. Believe it or not, there are even some creeps who aren't academics."

"Yes, but why would the murder scene be a second-floor office in Loomis Hall? If it was at all premeditated, someone would have had to get Les up there. Who else but a department member would say, for example, at such and such time, meet me in or in front of Gary Hake's office? It has to be an 'inside job.' That's what your friend Amos Herschberger, gentleman alpaca farmer and campus rent-a-cop said."

He responded to my grimace, "Hey, I don't mean to poke fun at Amos. His herd of two dozen alpacas already makes him a big Ohio breeder. Anyway, doesn't Gary lock up every Monday before your meeting? Who else has keys but you guys? And" he grinned knowingly, "one special friend.

"Mary Best," he added. "if you broke rules to give me my own key, who's to say that everyone else in the department hasn't broken the same rule? I know Les kept dropping hints about having a key. Once he told me he'd broken the key barrier. I had no idea at the time what he was talking about. But even if he did have a key, he's the one person who is not a suspect!"

Tony turned for a second so he could continue to talk to me and face Gus, who was waiting for our order. His smile was for Gus: "That garlic and tomato smell is going to my head. If that's The Tuesday Night Special, we'll have it, please," as if Gus didn't know.

"Well, Tony, maybe Les did unlock the door himself. But the possibility exists that maybe someone unlocked the door for him. That someone had to know that Gary's office would be empty, that all the offices along the corridor would be empty because of the regular Monday faculty meeting. Of course, the meeting's no secret. But O.K., let's act or, I mean, think on the premise of guilt limited to the department for a while. I'm out as a suspect and you, as sort of a step-member of the department, are out too. And certainly poor Les is out . . . permanently. So whom does that leave?"

Tony interrupted me with a laugh, "This is who. We have to list every member of the department, each alibi, and all motives. Who could even have a motive? I'm sure no one here knew Les before he came on campus this Fall. Les has said as much. Hon, do you have any idea what leads the professionals are following? I've heard that when they counted visible and latent prints, everyone's fingerprints were on the paperweight."

"Sure," I countered, "everyone's fingerprints would have to be on it. Everyone in the department nervously moved it around when called in to Gary's office, where the position of his visitor's chair puts each prof. in front of his desk and literally on the carpet. Did I ever tell you that he purposefully had his own desk chair made higher so that he's always looking down on the poor penitent or petitioner on the other side?"

Tony concluded, "Everyone's fingerprints on the paperweight are just as bad as no fingerprints, especially since they say there's no way to date any of the prints. What did good, old 'Just Call Me Seth' and the police say when you talked with them?"

At that moment a contrapuntal laugh and some singing from the next table unintentionally underscored Tony's question. Maybe Our Place wasn't the best place to have a private conversation, I thought as I picked what seemed like the one hundreth olive out of my pasta. I realized I should have asked some questions about The Tuesday Night Special, after all! I waved my fork in Tony's general direction and said, "Cut it. Seth is much smarter than you give him credit for. He gets a lot of mileage out of that 'I'm just a hick cop' role, but there's a pretty sharp mind under that Midfield haircut."

"O.K., O.K., Mary Babe," Tony wiped some marinara sauce off of his fingers before he patted me on the shoulder. "We're both getting wound up. We've got to relax and try to take one day at a time." He let his fingers linger.

"I'll try, Tony-hon, but lately I've been feeling as if several days have ganged up and been attacking me at once."

Tony smiled his agreement and thought out loud, "I wish we had more facts. I saw the fingerprint team come in as we were leaving yesterday. That was odd. What good would dusting for prints be after fifteen or twenty people have been milling around? Do you think that we -No, it was only me." I restrained my English teacher-self.

"Do you think that I was the only one who touched the body? Maybe between the time we first found the bodies and the time the police showed up no one else touched anything in Gary's office, but later the whole corridor and other offices were jammed with people. Some must have gone into Gary's space too. Any earlier footprints and fingerprints would have been obliterated. Why did they dust all of those offices anyway? It's useless." In his frustration, Tony actually started to create engineering masterpieces of knives and forks.

Refusing to be drawn into a fingerprint argument that was the realm of professionals, I went back to what we had made our own problem. "Look, Tony, why are we insisting that Gary's office had to be empty? Why couldn't Gary have asked Les to meet him there and killed him? But why would he? He really doesn't have a motive outside of his general meanness. And I don't think Victoria would let him."

"Who's Victoria?"

I just shook my head. I couldn't expect Tony to keep all of the campus romances straight. I couldn't myself. But he had met Victoria, I explained. "Victoria Sicard's that pretty

Spanish teacher in the Romance Language department. Vickie and Gary have been an item for years. In fact, ten years ago they thought they were on the cutting edge of Midfield's avant garde social life when they started to live together over on Morton St. You know, that wonderful 1852 Gothic Revival house? It was a shock when they found that no one cared then; certainly no one cares now. I don't think they care all that much about each other either. But they're stuck with their 'oh, so contemporary' lifestyle, and even more with the house they invested plenty in. Preservation doesn't come cheap. Once in a while, they still work together as a team and with combined goals can throw heavy tenured power around. I've seen them frighten students, I suppose weaker faculty too, with their cross-discipline, good prof, bad prof routine."

Tony pushed his plate away to add with emphasis, "I do know some campus gossip, Mary Beth. Didn't I hear that Victoria is interested in Les's fiancee Margarita Berenguer? There, you have a motive."

"I don't think it's a motive, Tony." I shook my head again. I seem to emphasize my remarks with a limited range of body language. "If it is a problem, it's just Victoria's. And maybe Gary's. Margarita was devoted to Les. And he to her. He always called Margarita Maria his favorite M&M."

"Did she melt-in-the-mouth, not in-the-hand, or is that disgusting under the circumstances?" Tony snickered at my raised eyebrow, sign of disapproval. "Oh, now I remember Victoria," he exclaimed. "That's Vic. She stopped by Loomis Hall Monday night to see what all of the excitement was about. When she found out, she complained bitterly that if the school scheduled a memorial service this week, she'd have to have an extra Botox treatment for a public ceremony.

"But, O.K., as much fun as they are to talk about, let's leave the subject of Gary and Vic for tonight. Let's move to a practical subject: Loomis Hall Geography 101. I've had too much red wine, Mary Beth. And I don't spend very much time in Loomis. So you go on and list the offices in order for me, hon."

Mr. Engineer Tony should be better at making diagrams than I was, I griped. But it wasn't worth an argument. I tore some sheets from the back of a workbook in my backpack and started listing. "Well, after Gary's, the next office is Stew's. W. Stewart Jones's to be exact. He won't tell anyone what the 'W' stands for. Maybe that's it," I joked. "Maybe Les found out and threatened to blackmail him. Maybe I've had too much Valpolicella too, Tony. But proximity to the crime doesn't necessarily make Stew the perpetrator. That's the office the Detective who we 'just call Seth.'" (I smiled), "and his police force are using for a Command Center."

I alternated fork use, first for another bite or two of the outstanding, now olive-less, pasta special, then for punctuation, as I explained, "Stew was close to Les, at least academically, and was giving him some advice on his doctoral dissertation. But that's all I know, except that Stew really is clever and funny. And not very strong. He uses humor to deflect academic problems and his colleagues' criticisms. But, hey, it's effective. And I know he still publishes obscure articles based on his own dissertation. In fact, all of the intellectual respect that he gets is based in those articles. His humor helps in teaching too; he's well known as the only person in the department who can point out Chaucer's dirty jokes and make him interesting to today's MTV generation."

Tony smiled to himself and added, "But he has to be the one making the jokes. He brought his bike over to the shop one day last week and complained to me that it handled funny. I told him that I'd tell the bike to straighten up and be serious. Didn't get a rise out of him."

"I think it's funny, Tony. But let's go on with the diagram: The next office used to be Roger Christian's. That's the one they were finally decent enough-or ashamed enough-to give to me. Roger is the guy who is always whining or laughing too loudly about something to get attention. He thinks he has to remind people he's still around because he is on loan to administration now and wants to get back into the department. At the least, he wants to have his vote counted as a member when it comes to new hires. He's desperate about it. He's also been terribly nervous lately. Have you noticed all of that twitching? I don't know what that's all about or why he wants to be reinstated in the department. I do know that he wanted to be able to vote for Les to be a permanent member of the department. Gary was fighting it. But what does that mean? That everyone has a reason to hate Gary. If he had been killed we would have plenty of suspects."

I continued my Loomis Hall map: "That leaves the part-timers' group office and Charlie's towards the end of the hall, unfortunately next to mine. Every time I come in or out, there he is, leaning against his door grinning, or is it leering, at me. I never would have had a large office there with a better view than his if I weren't here on a temporary assignment. Believe me, I would have had to work my way up, square foot by square foot. But two years as Visiting Professor might not seem so tentative to some. You don't think that I'm next, that someone would kill me for my office, do you Tony? Right after the police appropriated their offices for 'Crime Scene' and 'Command Center,' Gary and Stew took over the part-timers' office, moved out most of the desks, and told the 'lesser' faculty to headquarter themselves in the library or staircases until the crime was solved."

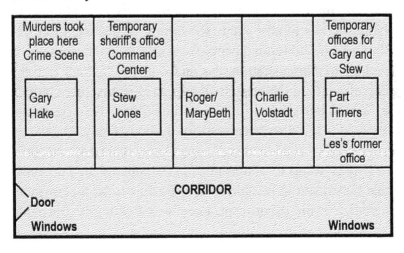

Murders took place here Crime Scene	Temporary sheriff's office Command Center			Temporary offices for Gary and Stew
Gary Hake	Stew Jones	Roger/ MaryBeth	Charlie Volstadt	Part Timers
				Les's former office
Door		CORRIDOR		
Windows				Windows

Gus looked over my shoulder while serving us coffee, the bill, and his version of art criticism. I was flattered when he recognized the schema I had drawn for the corridor it was supposed to represent.

Tony interfered with my creative glow. "Do you know what I think, Mary Babe? I think we'd better call it a night. We can do some investigating on our own and get back to detecting together in a day or two. Remember? Tomorrow's my Internet copyright law class."

I keep forgetting that Tony has a life, too! He needed some time to wipe his mind clean of Les and Krypto and to concentrate on legally protecting himself from those *Bartlett's Quotation* people. Bartlett's his name, too. He ought to be able to use it for his book title. Though, I have to admit, that name he shares is going to help sell his book.

We walked most of the way together to our separate living quarters. Sometimes I agree with Tony, it seems silly to keep up two establishments, especially since I have the whole first floor of the old Siebenschuh home. Old Mrs. S's belongings are stored upstairs while her heirs fight over what they want to do with the property. But I'm afraid that, as much as Tony thinks that he wants to live with me, he'd probably go berserk in a week. Less. I try to be neat while he's around, but as it is, at times I'm so eager to get into bed with him that I'm ready to drop my clothes on the floor wherever we are. He's the one who gets up in the middle of the night and puts them on hangers in the closet.

Could such a deliberately methodical engineer permanently put up with my spilling, tossing, and dropping? What about my highly personal method of organization? All books of fiction and poetry that don't fit in the bookcases are stacked asymmetrically on my bedroom floor; all reference books and clippings form patterns on the living room floor; journals are in the bath, and so on. I'm aware if even a brochure has been moved, but anyone taking one look at the leaning tower of papers that dominate my home-cum-office would never guess that. Most people make the mistake of confusing order with neatness. But I think Tony is beginning to recognize that you can have one without the other.

Even though lately our pillow talk has changed from our private sex code to our own private eye's code, Tony is gradually turning his small apartment over the bike shop into his publishing office and spending five out of seven nights at my house-keeping both of us happy.

Chapter Ten

*"We catched fish and talked, and we took a swim
now and then..."*

Mark Twain, Adventures of Huckleberry Finn, 1884

ॐ

Since I've been in Midfield, I've tried and pretty well
succeeded in swimming three times a week. I find a half-mile
swim is a good tonic for stress release and for problem
solving. The pool is good for my morale too. It's not just that
everyone tells me how terrific I look in a tank suit, but rather
that water is my true medium. It's the one place where I'm
graceful, and that's not because, as Tony insists, swimming
laps isn't conducive to carrying anything I could drop.

A little discipline is required to set aside regular times;
I'm so easily distracted here with my home and place of
work being just about interchangeable. But Midfield
Campus College makes it easy for me. The college is in its
second year of a faculty health kick, encouraging all faculty

members to participate in sports and use the campus facilities. As a result of the school's still new health program, the pool is reserved two hours daily for faculty swim. If I don't have a meeting, I always choose the noon swim on Mondays and Fridays. But on Wednesday, 6 a.m. is my hour of choice. Even though swimming laps is an individual sport, Wednesday has become my small group day. I've gotten into the habit of swimming then with my two new good friends, and personal campus grapevine, Abby MacKenzie, Medical Examiner, and Janet Purlis, the wife of Curley Purley. Janet is an excellent craftswoman and one of the few faculty wives I really like. In addition to our 'small group swim,' Janet and I have an off-campus lunch with Abby once a week and take turns having each other and spouses (in my case, almost-spouse) to Sunday brunch.

This Wednesday morning-only two days after the most horrible crime, the only crime, I'd ever been connected with-was no exception. In fact, Abby, Janet, and I felt we needed our swim and being together more than usual. Janet and I, of course, had talked on the phone most of Tuesday evening while she filled me in on what had happened during the *après*-chat with Curt and some of my colleagues. But those phone calls, as important as they were, didn't take the place of a face-to-face.

The three of us call ourselves 'The Sane Janes'; that's in contrast with everyone else at McCollege and the rest of the world. We usually spend as much time laughing as swimming, but not this Wednesday.

We greeted each other poolside with a few brief swim-talk words about the temperature of the water. The life guard posts air and water temp each day in resplendent colors on a white board at the far end of the pool. "Hey, Mary Beth," Abby called dangling one foot into the water, "it's 83 degrees today. Pretty good."

"And room temp is 80." Jan signaled across the pool, so I wouldn't have to go up to the white board to read it for myself.

"Great," I shouted making the simple adjective combine a greeting to my two friends with an approval of the water temperature. "Remember last week when it was 79? Anything below 80 and it takes me about ten laps to warm up." Swimmers can watch and feel the difference of one degree in water temperature the way an anxious new mother watches the thermometer and feels one degree of fever on baby's forehead.

It took me about a half-hour to swim my 36 lengths. That is, I think I swam the usual 36. I was so busy trying to get a clearer picture of Les's and Krypto's murders that I sometimes lost count. But it must have been the full half-mile because I finished at just about the same time Abby and Jan did. The three of us showered and met again in the locker room where the conversation (or yelling over the noise of the hair dryers) started out by following the usual pattern of our Wednesday girl-friend swim chats: Jan, who was starting to braid her magnificent coil of prematurely gray hair, said as she does every week, "One of these days I'm just going to cut my hair and wear it like yours, Mary

Beth. It's so much easier for swimming. And you always look terrific."

Abby completed the ritual by saying as she does every week, "Oh, if my hair would turn a beautiful gray like yours, Jan, I'd keep it that way. But I found three frizzy gray hairs this week and I think I should start to dye my hair."

Once these opening ritualized speeches were over, everyone was ready for my un-prefaced, "Well, what do you think?" Jan and Ab knew what I was asking about. In concert they demonstrated their seriousness by turning off their hair dryers.

Abby stalled for a little more thinking time, "10-9 as our new buddy Deputy Miller would say. Repeat the question, Mary Beth."

"What do you think?" I queried again.

Janet stopped a minute for a drink of her favorite imported water, then spoke, "No. What do you think, Mary Beth? I've given you all of the real information I have, even if it was limited to Tuesday's *après*-chat. But you found the body. You have contact with more of the potential suspects. Level with us. We've heard every wild rumor on campus. And they are wild-everything from you're a suspect yourself, Mary Beth, to the Rev. Al Sharpton's coming to town."

Abby looked to make sure no one else was in the locker room. "I'm not speaking out of turn," she said, "because plenty of people talk about this on campus. It's the most common rumor. I'm not going to breach confidentiality by giving names of students who have complained to the Wellness Center. But you do have one person in your department, Mary Beth, whose general character is suspect."

"Do you mean Charles Volstadt?" I asked as I rinsed my suit in the prescribed cold water. "He's let me know he's available when Tony drops me. Flattering, isn't it!"

"Yes, Charlie. Not exactly your type, Mary Beth, though he's known for his roving eye. And students have complained of his roving hands, too." Abby wrung her suit out unconsciously illustrating her personal punishment for sexual harassment.

"But, girls, a strong, non-discriminatory sex drive doesn't equal a murderer. Certainly if he's been preying on young women in his classes, he should be kicked out or be the recipient of some disciplinary action. You don't have any proof of harassment, do you, Abby?" Jan took another drink from her omnipresent water bottle.

"No, Jan, not yet, but he has had a conference with the Dean of Faculty about it. Actually, that was at the end of the summer. I'm not sure if you were even on campus yet, Mary Beth. I do think he might have changed his ways. But what if he hasn't? He's the only one in the whole department who has a publicly questionable character. I think we should look into his possible motivations and opportunities."

"He bought a four strand necklace with an antique Chinese jade pendant on it from me a few months ago," Janet added. "Now that I think about it, he really blushed when he told me it was for his mother. Do you think that's significant? Or do you think it hurts his Lothario image to be seen buying jewelry for a parent?"

Following her own line of thought, Abby said, "Whoever the killer is, he'll never get away from you by taking a water route, Mary Beth. You sure were swimming in the fast lane this morning. Saying that makes me wonder: are any of those English guys living in the fast lane? That could be a motive. We all probably have our own opinions about who the killer is. We should have some facts to check those opinions against as soon as the results come in from the DNA test Sheriff Yoder (I just can't 'call him Seth') asked for."

"DNA?" I was thoughtful. "DNA. That's not what John Donne was thinking of when he used the phrase 'eloquent blood' but it's certainly an apt description. He even used it as part of a funeral elegy ' . . . her pure and eloquent blood/Spoke in her cheeks, and so distinctly wrought/That one might almost say her body thought.'"

"You're spending too much time with Tony," Jan interrupted. "He's not always a good influence. Remember how embarrassed you were the first time he met your Dean? Instead of 'hello' like any normal person would say, your Tony had to strike a pose and theatrically declaim Sir Richard Burton's, 'Why meet we on the bridge of Time to 'change one greeting and to part.'"

Abby gave her a significant look that shifted conversational gears back to solving the crimes. The two of them had been good friends before I came to Midfield; they communicated on many levels. I could see they had passed some kind of nonverbal messages between them. It was particularly noticeable since they both turned to me at the same time. Spokeswoman Janet said, "Mary Beth, we think you are the one to investigate Charlie."

Abby added, "You belong in Loomis Hall. You belong in the offices of the English department, especially," she laughed, "now that you've got your office in with the big boys instead of at the Buck."

Janet struck a pose and issued an order, "Case the joint, Mary Beth."

Abby was laughing so hard, she could hardly get out "*D'accord.* I agree. Give one of us a call tonight and let us know what you've found out. What would Tony say: It's now or never. Sink or swim. Cut bait or catch fish?"

Jan and Abby struck up a chorus, "Go, girl, go. Go, girl, go."

I pulled on my jeans and sweater. I went.

Chapter Eleven

"Singularity is almost invariably a clue".

*The Boscombe Valley Mystery, Sir Arthur Conan Doyle,
1859-1930*

෭෨

Wednesday classes let out early at Midfield College.
Campus lore says that the founders or someone along the line
had expected that most graduates would be respectable
professionals, doctors (or barbers, I mused) who automatically would take Wednesday afternoons off. They might as
well get in the rhythm of it as undergraduates.

So Wednesday afternoon was usually my laundry
afternoon. Today, with crimes to solve and classes to prepare,
I thought I'd skip lunch and use the time for my favorite
household tasks. It was almost a luxury to wash and dry in
the new first-floor laundry room poor Mrs. Siebenschuh
had added just before she died. What was I thinking?
Household tasks? In anyone's scheme of things, a murder

would rank higher than laundry. I ignored the towels, sheets, clothes, (were there some books in that tangled mixture?) tumbling out of the over-filled laundry basket and decided to bike into town to see if I could find "Just Call Me Seth" in his regular office.

I admired my Raleigh's USA fade colors as I pushed it down the green painted steps and hopped on to begin my Seth search. I thought it might be hard to find him as he commuted between his Command Center at Loomis, his official space in the County Court House on Main Street, and the County Jail on Liberty. A jail? On Liberty? Some of our forefathers and foremothers must have had a macabre sense of humor. In fact, I hoped it would be hard to find him as I was enjoying the ride with my new soft saddle and high handle bars. It was a glorious day and a typically flat, Ohio drive into town. I had no need to play with the seven speeds Tony had forced me to finally master. I almost regretted finding Seth at my first stop, behind his own desk. My almost regret was short lived; Seth seemed glad to see me. "Let's have some coffee, Mary Beth, and home-made cookies."

The coffee did smell good, but I've read enough detective stories to know that station house coffee is supposed to be just this side of mud. Seeming to read my mind, Seth said, "We grind and brew our own arabica beans here at the Midfield Sheriff's Department. It's one of our community services. Any Midfieldian is invited to stop by any time, day or night, for a cuppa and an informal chat with his friendly, neighborhood officer. Small town living has some advantages," he laughed.

When we moved from coffee to Les, it turned out that Seth had prepared more questions for me than I had for him. Well, it was his job, whereas I knew darn well that I had a lot to learn even to be an amateur detective.

Was my face red as I tried to explain my sleuthing skills (or lack of) to Seth. I did not mention Abby and Jan's orders to me. I just told Seth that I had prowled around Charlie Volstadt's office earlier in the day when I knew he was teaching his Victorian Lit class. A cautionary tale in itself! How could I have known that this would be the day Charlie had chosen to give his students a library assignment? I only hope that when he caught me at his door, he thought I was going in, not coming out. My pulse was pounding so hard, I swear he could hear it.

"Just looking for you, Charlie," I had gasped. At least the gasp was sincere. I did find out that Charlie drinks a lot, as I told Seth, continuing to report the incident somewhat sheepishly to him. "I see him drinking at parties and meetings, but everyone in the department has an occasional beer or glass of wine. He drinks more than most, though I didn't realize it might be a problem until I saw all of the dead beer and wine bottles stashed away in his office, way too many for normal office use. I can't believe that I didn't smell that alcohol mist before, especially since he always stands uncomfortably close when he's talking to me. He must wait until he has a couple of bags full of bottles, then takes them out, so they don't tarnish the Loomis Hall trash image for the social anthropology class." Seth's inquiring look at the phrase 'trash image' called for a brief explanation. After all, if you weren't part of this campus, how would you guess that in lieu of actual anthropological sites, the class digs through faculty office trash once or twice a month?

Then I remembered what Abby had said about sexual harassment and began to think over various incidents that showed Charlie is not the proper person he tries so hard to make us believe he is. A secret drunk? Even a letch? Why not? When no one else is around, his remarks to me are pretty obvious. But is his being a drunk a consideration? I'd talk with Seth about it later. Charlie was also a failed writer. Everyone in the department knows about his attempts to get his books and short stories published. He had been kicked out of the Wednesday Writers Workshop, a sometimes serious writing group whose members meet weekly on campus to criticize each other's work. That might be his reason for drinking so heavily, but it's hardly a reason for murder, I reasoned. Wouldn't Tony be proud of me for remembering that it was Gore Vidal who wrote, "Teaching has killed more good writers than alcohol"?

Seth didn't seem a bit averse to giving me information. So I pushed, "Seth, are you considering only people from the English department?"

"Yes, Mary Beth, at least at this time. As a matter of fact we did look into Curt Perlis from the Chemistry department, that blonde guy you call Curley Purley," he said laughing.

"I know that he had befriended Les. But we think it was because Les is black. It seems that Perlis has a reputation for being a mentor to any minority student who will have him. I was told that he's so busy being liberal that he can't keep up. Sometimes he has to dump one minority student for the newer one on campus. He might have been ready to dump Les."

We keep getting these motives in reverse, I thought. This one is a provocation for Les to kill Curley Purley, not for Curley to kill him. But it's hardly a motive at all!

Seth, reading my mind, again, went on. "We don't have to worry about a motive though because Perlis's alibi completely checks out. He was at the American Chemical Society (ACS) giving a paper that reportedly manages to relate his research to Lewis's *Lives of the Cell*, then to Euclid. Everyone remembered it! He gave the study on a Sunday evening panel. It caused such a stir that he had to have a follow-up discussion meeting on Monday. The pathologist's report is specific. No room for doubt. Monday is when Les was killed, though he hasn't pin-pointed the exact time yet. So we're really back to members of your department, Mary Beth."

Seth went on talking and I went on half listening, not a good trait in a would-be detective, when I heard him say something that I had to ask him to repeat. "Yes. I'm asking you to help us, Mary Beth. Not in any official capacity, of course. I'm the lead officer-the only officer working on these crimes. Deputy Dwayne Miller is taking care of any other Midfield problems while I put in full time on this murder. I'm not commissioning you as another deputy sheriff or assistant detective, nothing as specific or important as that. But I can use you. I'll tell you, by the time I listened to Charlie's and Roger's," Seth paused and looked at his notes, "'privileged signifier' and 'constructs of subordinacy in binary opposition,' I realized that listening to them was like trying to read my doctor's handwriting. I firmly believe that no suspect says absolutely nothing, but sometimes nothing is all I can get from your department's jargon. I need help here in translating academic English into real English. I've done as thorough a background check on you as you're ever going to get, Mary Beth."

I was sure he had. Information on campus travels faster than it would in any chat room. Abby had already told me that Janet had told her that Purley told her that his tennis partner (Roger? Charlie? Stew? I wondered which one it could have been) told him Gary had reported to Seth that I was the only possible suspect. I was new on campus, had, in fact, appeared when Les had. If that isn't suspicious, what is? And, he pointed out, I kept to myself. Well, no one asked me any place those first few weeks. Gary, himself, had been as interested in being seen with me socially as he was in having his hair grow out gray. All in all, what Gary reported to Seth was that I was a very suspicious person. So Seth's informing me of a background check made me wince a bit, but didn't come as much of a surprise.

"I've watched you carefully these past two days," Seth explained. "And I trust you; that is, I trust you with deciphering and minor snooping. This isn't standard operating procedure, Mary Beth, but in the case of these McMurders, I'm going to need some knowledgeable eyes and ears on Campus. Your campus isn't far from downtown, but it's like entering a foreign country for most of us Midfielders." Was I flattered. But was I too flattered to distinguish the line I shouldn't cross, the line between enjoying my role as girl detective and probably enjoying just as much the role of spying on my friends? Not I, I reassured myself. I would be doing research work.

Cops R Us. I committed myself and eagerly told my now-colleague Seth the rest of my theories. We had discussed Charlie, so that left Roger and Stew and Gary. It was next to impossible to think that anyone I worked with could murder an animal, let along a human being. No one seemed to have any motive either. All have character flaws, but who doesn't? If it weren't for the crimes, the flaws wouldn't even be apparent except for Charlie's well-hidden alcoholism and not-so-well-hidden attraction to his women students.

Even though I joined the majority in not caring for Gary, what could I accuse him of-incivility? Extreme rudeness coupled with extreme ambition is not a crime, though like any other vice, if exaggerated enough, it could lead to crime. What did Stew ever do wrong? So, he procrastinates. Don't we all? I know procrastination is my failing, one of my failings! Plus, Stew has the advantage of being clever and funny. He can usually hide his stalling with a few witty disclaimers and do what he wants when he wants. And

Roger? What a joke. Though I suppose that weak people murder sometimes just out of frustration. And his whole life was a frustration. From the beginning, he had to bear the surname Christian when he liked to think of himself as an Agnostic; his first choice of Atheist would have been a little too strong for Midfield's church going community. "And'" he would invariably add, "'Atheists don't have any holidays." He would continue his religious explanation by bragging, when he wasn't whining, that he was the only Christian in Midfield whose Sunday morning ritualistic ceremony consisted of going down to the drugstore to buy the *New York Times*.

"But they are all so predictably eccentric," I said to Seth. "That's what academia does to you, especially in a small town where there's no place else to go."

"On the other hand," I remembered, "Some were a tad peculiar before they were drawn to Midfield. Look at Stew's dissertation. They all still tease him about it. It's an analysis of *The Raj Response to Comparative Grammars of the Modern Aryan Languages*. That was for his graduate degree, so you can't blame Midfield or the College for all of his oddities. And Charlie's reputation didn't start here either. Present company excluded," I added modestly, "McCollege doesn't draw its staff from the top tier of U.S. professors."

"So I've been told, Mary Beth. The report is that your department's hiring process is extremely cumbersome and convoluted, resulting in some odd hires. But I have to say that the way Les Delaney and Gary Hake went about straightening out the process perplexes me. It just doesn't sound right.

"But you're off to a good start," my new boss encouraged me. "Think a little more; look a little more. That boyfriend of yours, he's pretty savvy about academics. I looked at his transcript. He's pretty savy about a lot of things. Talk to him about it, too." As if he didn't know that I talked with Tony every day.

Chapter Twelve

"Chance favors only the prepared mind."

Louis Pasteur

૨ઌ

I was almost too proud about my new assignment from Seth, certainly a promotion from taking surveillance orders from Abby and Jan. Puffed up with new importance in the hitherto unknown field of crime detection, I started back across campus with the intent of picking up campus mail on my way home. The campus looked beautiful, I reflected, with red and yellow autumn leaves shining against the still green grass. And I was feeling on top of everything. But within a few minutes I had lost some of my hubris and was shaking my swimmer-friendly haircut in self-reproachful anger. Sure, I'd told my new buddy Seth everything I could think of, everything Tony and I could think of, everything Abby, Janet, and I could think of. But what had he told me? I started to make a mental list of items discussed. Maybe next time around I would hand him a typed list of questions to be answered. Or would that be too presumptuous? For example, I wasn't even sure if the police were certain that Les was the intended victim. What if someone had come to that office meaning to murder Gary, plenty of motivation there, and Les just happened to be at the very wrong place at the very wrong time?

Speaking, or thinking, of the devil: There was Gary's Burberry hat with Gary underneath it. He was striding toward me, bulking large on the one-lane path I was taking to my office, which means he was just leaving his. Now that I was facing him, I felt so guilty at what I had been thinking about him that I tripped, caught myself, but dropped all of my books.

"Hey, Mary Kay," he called as he approached. I knew I was stepping into something, so I gathered up my books and courage and dared to correct him, by saying, "It's Mary Beth, Gary."

"Oh" he grinned, walking around my strewn books and papers with exaggerated fastidiousness, "I meant Mary K., for klutz."

Stunned, again, I could think of nothing stronger than an under my breath, "Get a life, Gary." Was he sitting up all night thinking of nasty remarks to make to me or was he just a spontaneous 'wit'? I always thought of come-backs later. I'd worked on a great gibe I planned to use some day, "Gary, please re-clothe that last remark in sesquipedalian iambics," except that I could never remember how to pronounce 'sesquipedalian'!

With renewed vigor I went back to thinking of Gary as the intended victim. Or maybe he was the murderer. Or what? He must be guilty of something!

And after the fact, as always, I thought of more questions I should have asked Seth. I had been so excited at thinking of myself as a semi-official detective that I had forgotten to ask what forensic evidence the crime lab had found when members of the English department were called in one by one on Monday. Had Seth counted on his collegiality making me more eager to talk than to ask the questions I had come prepared to push just a few hours ago?

"What?" I was so busy walking along and mentally making my list, I hadn't even noticed our favorite waiter Gus in his daytime job as art department student until he was almost on top of me.

"I was just saying, 'Hey, Dr. Valpolicella.' Say, how did you like the flower arrangement on your table last night? I'm combining my vocation as art history major and avocation as waiter by copying famous floral arrangements, I mean, as long as they're only one or two stems, for the restaurant tables." And last night my mind had been so occupied with poor Les's murder that I thought someone had robbed a cemetery. "Tuesday night," he continued, "was my interpretation of Marsden Hartley's 'Lilies'. Mr. and Mrs. Marquis de Riscal said it-"

I interrupted, "When you called me Dr. Valpolicella and the restaurant owners Mr. and Mrs. Marquise de Riscal, does that mean you remember what each of your regular customers drinks?"

"Of course it does, Dr. Valpolicella. I've got a great memory and I put it to practical use. I mean it earns me good grades at the college and terrific tips at Our Place."

"Are you saying that if I gave you a list of everyone in the English department, you could write down-"

"You've got it. Like, I don't even need any extra time to write down anything. Just tell me a name and I'll tell you what he drinks. I'm kind of a human vinificator," he giggled, "an idiot savant about wines and who drinks them."

"Les Delaney"

"Hey, you know Les was only part-time faculty and still a graduate student. He didn't have money to, like, spend on bottles of wine at Our Place or any other restaurant. Sometimes when neither of us were working I'd get together with Margarita and he ('him', I couldn't help correcting) and we'd party with a six-pack or a supermarket bottle of vino tinto. Like, I mean no one cared about the brand, but it had to be under $7.00! That dude was trying to learn though. He read Our Place's old *Gourmet* magazines for the wine articles. I mean I'd save him a particularly mellow glass whenever I could. He said pretty soon he'd return the favor. But you know what? He had all of those allergies. I'm not sure he could always taste and smell the difference or if he just went by labels."

"Dr. Hake?""

Not much of a wine drinker. Usually has a sherry and a

vodka martini. His liver-inner, whatshername, I mean, Vic, joins him in the sherry, but then switches to whatever French white wine she thinks she can one-up me about. But, hey, this is Midfield, I mean how many exotic labels do you think we carry?"

"O.K., let's try Dr. Jones, Stew Jones?"

"Oh, he's a cab through and through. Cabernet Sauvignon, no Merlot blends. He really knows his wines and lets us know that our commercial brands aren't good enough for a true wine gourmet! Once in a while, like when he's entertaining, I let him bring in a few of his own bottles." Gus assumed what he clearly thought of as his sophisticated air, "I mean, not bad that Chateau Margaux."

"And Dr. Charles Volstadt?"

"He's a red wine, too. I call him Dr. Merlot, but he doesn't really care as long as his drink is smooth."

"Dr. Christian?"

"That's easy. It all starts with a 'c'. Christian and Dr. Chianti Classico. Pretty good, aren't I?"

"You are. Thanks loads, Gus. Looking forward to seeing your Georgia O'Keefe centerpiece next time." Half-teasing Gus and half-thinking he just might create a southwestern table arrangement, I thought I was ending the conversation.

"Wait, Dr. Goldberg. Do you have a minute? I know this isn't your real office hours or anything, but could I talk to you about me for a minute?"

I nodded a 'yes,' somewhat surprised as Gus isn't one of my advisees.

"I'm thinking of changing majors-actually more-leaving McCollege. Sorry, Professor," he apologized.

"That's O.K., Gus. 'McCollege' isn't a dirty word for me, though you're right to be careful. Go on, please."

"I'm getting more interested in wine than I am in art history and I've been reading up on viticulture. That's grape growing," he explained to me as one uninitiated and continued, "and oenology. That's wine making. I've been thinking of both of them as new majors. I don't want to go out to the University of California, but Ohio State has courses in wine analysis and practical wine-making workshops. I could take a couple of chemistry courses and make my own major. What do you think?"

"Wow, Gus. My first thought is that I would miss seeing you on campus. Why don't you discuss this with your advisor and keep all of your options open. You don't have to decide now. Apply to Ohio State; that's one of your options. But let's think about it for a while. Make an appointment and come talk with me in a couple of weeks."

"Thanks loads, Professor G. One thing I know is that it's a huge job market. Graduates in oenology can get great jobs right here in the U.S. wine and grape industries. Ohio has about 50 wineries. Who would've thunk it?"

"Does Gus's information mean anything or not?" I would ask Tony when I phoned him later that afternoon. Of course, it depends on what the forensics team found on the corkscrew or if you can even tell one cork from another or if wine drinkers stay 100% true to their viniferous selves.

I stopped for a minute at the student bookstore to pick up some green pens. My plans for that night were to read and comment on student journals, an activity I had previously dreaded, but now seemed so orderly and promising. Not at all like the wine drinking habits of my colleagues, which will probably turn out to be useful only in deciding what bottle to bring to a party! I like to write my comments to my students in green ink. If I write in black or blue, it's hard at first glance to tell my comments from theirs. If I write in red, it's threatening. All of them have been in school long enough to associate red ink with bad news. Green seems neutral and visible, encouraging them, I hope, to read and be influenced by my responses.

One more stop before the promised peace of home. I picked up the few letters that were stuffed into my box along with the overflow of junk mail. It seems everyone from the Modern Language Association to the Ohio Writers' Conference wants me to renew my membership. One interesting memo was almost tossed out with the lot, a surprising memo from Stew: "Mary Beth-Would you consider team teaching my Colonialism class next semester? We could add your interpretations of Forster's *A Passage to India* and Lowry's *Under the Volcano* to my take on *Memoirs of a Bengal Civilian* and Kipling's *Kim*. How about it? It's a fun class, M.B. You'll like it and the students will like you. Stew." I could feel my face breaking into a grin of victory as I happily mused about Stew's memo. Was this another part of my new notoriety or had I passed some unknown initiation test and was, so to speak, arriving in my department?

Stew's request plus the small success of being able to traverse the few blocks to my house without dropping more books brought me smiling to my retreat. Retreat? With a telephone, cell phone, computer, fax, and answering machine! Anyone could reach me. But, no one did. So the imp of the perverse struck again: I had come home to be alone, but now that I was home, I wanted to be with people. I felt a certain energized benevolence I wanted to share with my colleagues. And I felt hungry. I'm not a good lunch-skipper. If I hurried I could still make the faculty dining room before it closed for those two emaciating hours between late lunch and early dinner.

Chapter Thirteen

"Oh, my friends, be warned by me,/That breakfast, dinner, lunch and tea/Are all the human frame requires . . . /"With that the wretched child expires."

Hilaire Belloc 1870-1953

🍂

The faculty dining room is one of the university's last unexplored frontiers of class striation. To the outsider it is as welcoming as an English garden; to the newcomer it is that impenetrable, rigid maze in the garden; to those who have taught a year or two, it is representative of the upstairs/downstairs system that keeps the garden verdant and enjoyed, especially by those with privileges.

I was fortunate that Caroline Mossberg had brought me into lunch the first couple of days I was at Midfield. Not that Caroline would have ever said anything as coarse as "this is where you should sit," but each of my first three days she had led me to the same table, the table where coincidentally, I innocently thought, all of the other new hires and part- timers were taking turns eating. By directing me to my true station, she saved me from making what for some was the fatal error of not recognizing class distinctions. I've heard whispered stories since then of he who tried twice to eat at the history table where dead silence greeted any of his comments, whether they were brilliant insights into the Civil War or ordinary social remarks about the day's temperature. I was warned that anyone who tries to put a tray down at the administration table is told, "This seat is taken," even if five empty chairs belie the claim. And try to pull up a chair at an occupied table for two. They still talk of the English department temp who had tried two years ago and literally had to write a note of apology. She was not rehired.

With no need to rush to afternoon classes, Maynard and Bettina, two of my new-on-campus buddies from the psych department, were taking their time over lunch. They were chatting excitedly. About the murders I thought. No. They were talking about the new student art work decorating the walls. The Faculty Senate had voted unanimously to replace the showing of boring hotel-lobby genre landscapes with original work by art majors. Maybe the student works weren't professional, but they had a freshness and energy that was a pleasant, even invigorating, change.

I let my own creativity loose by organizing a salad from the salad bar to accompany the macaroni and cheese I had piled high on my plate. "That comfort food seems to have been the order of the day," I put my tray down, laughing so they would get the pun. From their blank faces, I could see an interpretation was needed, "Order? Order of the day." I pointed with my chin to the cheese encrusted plates left by the last lunch shift.

For a while we did what new faculty does best, compared notes on the student body, on what our expectations had been and what we found. We didn't discuss individual students; we were too highly principled for that. So we spoke in blithe generalities about our new academic life. We agreed that the students were of a pretty high caliber, but in general not risk-takers, that in our classes we had some artists and poets, but that they would not grow up to be artists and poets. In today's chilly academic economy, we were happy to be working, and pleased to be teaching students who were serious about their studies, liked to debate in classes, and whatdya know, had a good sense of humor, i.e. laughed at our jokes.

The students seemed to be taking Les's murder in their stride, we decided. "After all," Bettina pointed out, "Most of them hadn't even known him. This was his first semester on campus. All he'd been teaching was two comp courses. That's forty students who would have had any contact with him."

The three of us stopped in mid-conversation. We remembered at the same time: only two days ago, on Monday, Les had been sitting at this very table with us. He had come into the lunch room arguing loudly with Stew about two contemporary historians. Once in the room, they would have turned and gone to separate tables anyway, so we didn't think anything of it at the time. Today Maynard thought it might be important, though the potential importance of their argument was diminished by Stew's having an alibi and being one of Les's mentors. Plus, Bettina interjected, "Can you imagine Stew's getting angry enough to slap anyone, let alone murder him? It's impossible to visualize. Though my field is psychometrics. What do I know? I'm just a testing psychologist." She quipped, "I don't do psychological profiling!"

"You know what else is important?" Maynard added, "That we tell your friend Detective Yoder we had lunch with Les. The M.E. can pretty well pinpoint the time of death from the autopsied contents of the stomach, especially if they know what time Les actually had lunch. If they have his lunch hour as a starting point, they can figure the digestive process back to the hour of the murder and we all know Les's lunch hour on Monday to the minute." Maynard and Bettina were relieved to accept my offer to call Seth with the information and to give them a credit line. Like most people on campus, they liked to talk about the case, but didn't want to be involved.

Back at my house I started to read a few more student journals, but took a break in the middle of reading Amos Hershberger's. Our good-looking rent-a-cop audits my class through a program set up by the Town and Gown Committee to ease any possible tensions between Midfield, the town, and Midfield, the college. The program permits any adult resident of Midfield to audit one class a semester

without paying tuition. Very few Midfieldians take advantage of the offer, but it was on the books to demonstrate the College's desire to co-operate with the town. Amos, though, was diligent in his attendance, in completing his work, and, now that I thought of it, in asking me for student conferences. He had filled most of his journal with what he sees as the romance of alpaca breeding, noting that Ohio is the largest alpaca-raising state in the country with 250 farms. I had to give him credit for planning a Great Alpaca Ranch Tour of the eleven Northeastern Ohio farms. But I had to wonder about the many pages of his journal that were filled with speculations on personal relationships between students and teachers. Maybe Tony was right. Maybe Amos did have a 'thing' for me. He certainly is attractive, I thought. And intelligent. Would it be unprofessional for me to fix him up with Abby?

I stopped reading and romancing to call Tony for his input. I wanted some ideas about how to approach Seth with Maynard and Bettina's information. Tony was more excited than I expected about our remembering lunch with Les on Monday. "This will put a definite time on the murders, Mary Beth. Not that we're suspects, but it will be nice to have science on our side." He was impressed, too, when I told him of Gus's ability to put wine labels on his customers. Tony wondered with me if this waiter's trick for caging better tips could in any way help us find the killer. "I know the police took a wine cork as evidence from Gary's waste basket on Monday," he reasoned. "But Gary oils the wheels of your department with wine, Mary Beth. He must open a bottle a day. Well, see if Seth will tell you if they found out anything from the cork."

"We could have parallel investigating activities going on," I added. "While we're waiting to hear the cork report, Tony, how about socializing more with my colleagues. I'll bet if we can get anyone talking . . . "

"Get anyone talking?" Tony interrupted. "Can you get an English professor to keep from pontificating 24/7?"

"Tony, I'm serious. Let's 'do dinner.'"

"I could come straight from work," Tony replied in agreement, proudly adding, "The guys in other bike shops dress down, but Bob makes us wear jeans and sandals. I'll do you proud, Mary Babe."

With the double reward of an interesting phone call to make to Seth and a detecting dinner out, I started to whip through the waiting Forster class journals, though I always take time for my strong point: detailed responses to my students' comments. Barry Glass's journal made me stop and think. A meticulous student, he had taken time to research a Forster interview in the "Writers at Work" series. He had copied part of the interview in his journal for use in a future paper. And I copied it from him to show to Tony that night . . . .

The interviewer, "Is there a hidden pattern behind the whole of an author's work, what Henry James called, 'A figure in the carpet'?"

Forster looked dubious.
"Well, do you like having secrets from the reader?"
Forster: "Ah, now that's a different question."

Maybe Tony and I were missing that 'figure in the carpet'! First, my call to Seth. I looked for Seth's card and phoned him at his downtown office. He was in as good a mood as I was. When I told Seth I had some exciting information, he replied, "I'll show you mine, Mary Beth, if you'll show me yours first."

Maybe I didn't know Seth as well as I thought I did! But he was indeed interested in our faculty lunch and in what we had eaten. "Can you possibly remember what Les had for lunch on Monday?"

"Sure. It's not hard. Monday was swiss steak and gravy day or more likely it was mock swiss steak and mock gravy day. No one at the table would eat it. All four of us, Les and I, Maynard and Bettina, had huge salads from the salad bar accompanied by what we thought of as a hilarious discussion on declaring a national holiday in honor of the unnamed inventor-hero who had discovered the first salad bar. Who would have guessed . . . ?"

"Good remembering, Mary Beth. Can you go one step farther and remember who else was in the lunchroom at the time? Did you see Charlie or Roger, for example?"

"Why are you using Charlie and Roger as 'for examples,' Seth? Do you know something I don't?"

"Of course I know things you don't know, Mary Beth.

You might know more about *Passage to India* than I do. But, this is my job and over the years I've become pretty good at it."

Seth was right. I was so proud of my minor multi-tasking abilities that I'd almost forgotten who the real detective was. I'd almost forgotten the argument Les had with Stew, too. I post-scripted that bit of information, but had to diffuse it by adding that they seemed to be having an academic argument about the historian Steven Ambrose with two profs from the History department.

"Thanks, Mary Beth." Seth rattled some papers, presumably reports, next to the mouthpiece to signal that he had work to do. My interview time was up. "Your lunch information is really helpful. I'll pass it on to Dr. MacKenzie and the state lab. And I'll add Stew and Les's argument to the long list of arguments to be investigated in your contentious department.

"My own news is more of eliminating a clue than finding one. I did it through the B. C. I."

Seth intercepted my question. "I'll explain. I'll explain." He explained: "Obviously with Dwayne Miller now in charge of local crimes, your friend Dr. MacKenzie and I can't handle this case by ourselves. I called in help from the state, the Bureau of Criminal Investigation, B.C.I., to be exact. A town the size of Midfield can't afford to have its own state of the art crime lab. We need the B.C.I. Right off the bat, their lab told me to forget the cork as a clue. The analyst himself told me that no way can we get a print from

it. Now we'll see what he can do, MacKenzie, too, with your lunch information. I'll talk with you later." Seth hung up; I assumed he turned back to the papers he'd rattled at me.

Later that night when we were alone I could give Tony the answer to his request: "Find out what Seth knows about the wine cork." It wasn't the answer he had expected, but Tony is never disappointed if even a negative occasion gives him a chance to quote Shakespeare at me: "Oft expectation fails, and most oft there/Where most it promises."

But now I was running late and still had to change into clean, chalk-free black jeans and psych myself into my Ms. Sherlock Holmes mode. Come-Mary Beth-come! The game is afoot.

Chapter Foureen

"Variety is the mother of Enjoyment". (1826)

*"What we anticipate seldom occurs; what we least
expected generally happens."*
(1837)

Benjamin Disraeli, 1804-1881

❧

A half-hour later I met Tony at Our Place for a record-breaking second night during the same week. Joining us was the easiest person to ask out at the last minute, the only bachelor in the department, Charles Volstadt. Charles, we learned, is not a true, long-time bachelor, but rather a recent one. "It's been almost three years since Miriam divorced me," he growled with unexpected rancor. "Can you imagine? When I told her she had to choose between that rotten Rotweiler and me, she chose him!" He was on such an anti-dog and anti-wife roll that I couldn't follow all of his logic, if it was logic. "I hate all dogs," he went on as he vehemently emptied the breadbasket, "and that Rotweiler was the worst, a threat to everyone in the neighborhood and especially to me. He hated me as much as I hated him and his teeth looked a lot sharper than mine."

Lining up little pellets of Italian bread on the table and knocking them down, he caught his breath, smashed a few more bread pellets, and visibly controlled himself. "I might as well tell you because you're going to hear it from others, the dog wasn't the only reason for the divorce. Miriam objected to a relationship, a perfectly simple relationship, I was having with one of my students. She objected so strongly I was beginning to look at my office as a place where I could relax after my strenuous home life. Anyway, I'm better off now. Rita graduated. Miriam left. And I hope her dog has been impounded and gassed or whatever they do to rid communities of those beasts."

He was too angry to notice the look that passed between Tony and me. Could Krypto's death have been the first crime and Les's murder a cover-up? Even I had to admit that a doggy-hate crime was a pretty far stretch for explanation or motive. But the look we exchanged was definitely a "we'll talk about this later" look.

Tony and I wanted to stay with our problem-solving program, but somehow we had tapped into Charlie's need for confession and absolution. " . . . no student sex after Elaine," he was saying when I tuned in again. "That was only once, but it certainly cements a relationship. That's when the College made me get counseling or get out." He tented his fat fingers, "And, well, here I am," he unnecessarily post scripted.

Charlie punctuated this explanation with a forced laugh as he concluded by telling us of the College's zero tolerance restrictions on his sex life. Well, we wanted to know. But this was enough, and we quickly changed the subject. In fact, when Gus came over to ask if the three of us eating together was a plot to confuse his identification-by-wine process, Tony was moaning about his pre-published book. "Sometimes I think I'll put all the quotations for my reference book in a blender and see if a novel comes out instead." With a shrug Tony acceded to Charlie's choice of Merlot for all of us.

Gus kept hanging around until I realized he really had wired some petals together to make an O'Keefe-style close up of a flower for the table. He wasn't waiting to take our order, but rather for his well-deserved kudos, which I was happy to give him with a simple caveat. "Gus, your art nourishes the human spirit. We need it. But now we need other nourishment, too."

Tony ordered for the three of us. He skipped the usual menu choices to order our meal based on what was becoming our personal tradition-basing choice on the great smells of tomato, garlic, basil, and oregano coming from Our Place's kitchen. Though Tony had often confessed to me that the aroma he really likes is the one that greets him each day when he comes to work, that refreshing smell of bike-shop rubber, it hasn't dulled his instincts for recognizing what's best in restaurant food.

While we were waiting for our order, it wasn't very hard to get Charlie on the subject of the murder. The murder was only two days old and was still all that he and we were thinking about. He was so transparent and obviously innocent, I thought, that even discussing his alibi seemed natural. "Everyone knows that we found the bodies around 4:30 p.m.," I said to Charlie. "Tony was just coming from the bike shop where he had been defending himself to disgruntled customers for most of the afternoon, a perfect, though not very pleasant, alibi for murders that the coroner now says took place between 2:30 and 3 o'clock. I was in class discussing with my students the possibility that as the author of *A Room with a View*, E. M. Forster was playing with his homosexuality by describing his disguised self as the heroine Lucy of the novel. We couldn't have been more visible. What about you?"

I'd never seen Charlie look sheepish before. "I like to take a nap before faculty meetings," he explained. "They tend to exhaust me. There's not only a lot of wrangling, but you'll see, Mary Beth, after you've been here for a while, there's a tremendous pressure to be brilliant. And," he added modestly, "if I have a little rest, I usually am. I'm actually much better at wanton deconstruction than the rest of them."

I poured the wine and passed the zucchini sticks. Tony pushed. He had the nerve for a most personal probe, "Were you napping by yourself?" I lowered my head in embarrassment and used my detective skills to investigate the warp and woof of the tablecloth.

But the question didn't bother Charlie at all. He stopped dipping his bread in oil only long enough to reply, "From your mouth to God's ear, Tony. But unfortunately, yes, I was alone. No Rita-in-training . Even though I believe that sex is one of the most beautiful, natural, wholesome things that a good grade can buy, I've learned my lesson. I have no one but my alarm clock to verify my whereabouts.

"In the interest of full disclosure," he continued, "you should know that during my Rita interlude, I broke a sacred rule of Gary's and gave her a key to the corridor for, let's say, personal reasons."

"Oh, I took it back at the end of the affair," he answered before we could even voice the question.

Hey, this isn't the pathetically flirtatious Charlie from Loomis Hall and faculty meetings. This Charlie is really funny. Maybe "wanton deconstruction" and "from your mouth to God's ear" wouldn't get him any stand-up comedy gigs, but he made the extravagance of an extra dinner out all worthwhile, though his attitude toward dogs was exceedingly strange. When Gus finally got around to serving us, it was a pretty good dinner, too. Those odors that had greeted us on entering had translated into a new taste, a surprisingly good Midfield-Italian blend. We weren't dining on the cutting edge of a new cuisine, but Tony and I agreed that the Wednesday night chef was a few cooking schools above his apparently apprentice chef who worked Mondays.

Before we left Our Place, Charlie informed us that he wasn't the only key villain of the department. He had learned Tuesday afternoon that Curley Purley and Les had key access to Loomis corridor, too.

Tony and I kept my own breach of department rules to ourselves. But now we had keys properly owned by Gary, Stew, Charlie, Roger, and me and improperly owned by Tony, Les, Curley, and Charlie's ex-girl friend. I could stop feeling guilty for having broken a department rule, but I'd also have to stop using who had a key to Loomis as a determining factor for guilt or even suspicion.

Later that night at my house, I showed Barry Glass's Forster quote to Tony. Tony has never met a quotation he didn't like, but he was especially enthusiastic about this one: "Your literary friends have it right, Mary Babe. That's what we have to do-find the hidden patterns in Les's life, and in the lives of your buddies in the English department. If we look hard enough, we'll see that 'figure in the carpet.'"

Tony and I then decided that investigative work consisting of dining out and good conversation was a fun way to uncover these hidden patterns. In rapid order we made plans for lunch with Gary and another dinner appointment with Stew. When we called him, Roger actually liked the idea of afternoon tea; he's so happy to have us still connect him even peripherally with British lit. While we were at it, we threw in an appointment with Margarita. We had already made our weekly Sunday brunch plans with Curley and Jan Purley. We found we weren't being a bit intrusive;

everyone was eager to talk. With our enabling new-found intrepid teamwork or perhaps chutzpah, we called Seth. He, too, said he would look forward to dinner with us later this week, a big Saturday night out, "a change," Seth said "from my usual Saturday routine of dropping in on the Bacchus strip club to kick out all under-aged students."

Chapter Fifteen

"... a moveable feast"

Ernest Hemingway, 1964

❧

Our second investigative meal was a breakfast with Margarita Berengeur early Thursday morning. Margarita looked terrible-as if she had been crying for days. She probably had been.

Seated across from her at the almost clean Formica table in Midfield's tawdry coffee and donut shoppe, Tony and I started our own good-cop/bad-cop routine. It was my turn to be the bad guy, but I couldn't keep up the pose. Margarita was so happy to be with us and so distraught at the same time that I was overcome with guilt. With no family or friends of her own on campus, Margarita regarded Tony and me as good friends, certainly Les's good friends. While I had been looking at the murders as puzzles to be solved, Les's death, for her, was an unbelievable and unmitigated tragedy. I thought of myself as a young Jessica Fletcher; she thought of me and Tony, too, as shoulders to cry on. "I'm so glad you invited me to breakfast," she said. "No one will tell me anything. I know how much you academicians hate the word, but 'closure' is what I want, what I need."

Margarita's inane remarks were heartbreaking in their ordinariness. "What will I do? Les's clothes, even his food are still in my house. I don't want to be alone forever.

"As for Les, the one thing in life he wanted," she insisted "was to finish his degree. Isn't there such a thing as a, you know, posthumous degree?" Tony looked to me to answer. I had never heard of such a situation, but anything is possible in academia. Margarita pushed, "Les's dissertation is almost finished." She twisted her long black hair as she nervously pleaded, *Black vs. White in Melville and Poe*. I have his, you know, notes and stuff. I could finish it for him. It would mean so much to his family and to him.

"Yes." She answered the question I couldn't keep out of my eyes. "Yes, even now it would mean a great deal to him. Somehow I'm sure Les would know. And he wasn't just talking about obvious symbolism. One of his themes had to do with, you know, dominance and colonialism. That's why Stew was so helpful to him," she added with another twist of her hair.

Semi-hypnotized, I began to concentrate more on the twistings than the listening. I drifted back in time to hear Margarita say, " . . . I'll bet that Les is the only one who really read Stew's dissertation all the way through. He was pretty excited about it. Imagine, excited about a, you know, 30-year-old dissertation. Most Profs think of their graduate school work the way a famous star thinks back to her first porno film. You know, they don't want anyone to see their early attempts for acclaim. Well, I didn't read it; I just know Les was excited."

Twenty minutes earlier I had considered myself serenely in control. Now I was adrift in arcane areas of academia. The whole conversation with Margarita was veering into strange fields: Awarding a post mortem Ph.D.? One the dead recipient would somehow 'know' about? I had to get out of this breakfast.

"Margarita," I leaned forward, covered her hand with mine, looked directly into her eyes, and lied, "Margarita, that's a wonderful idea. You know Gary Hake well enough to know that he won't be sympathetic. Why don't you go straight to Vice President Mossberg and discuss it with her. If she can't help you, it's her job to tell you who can." I gathered steam, "I hate to run and leave you two like this, but I have to get ready for my nine o'clock class. I'll just take the other half of my English muffin with me. See you later."

I had a last minute thought. I opened my briefcase. Les's beige cardigan was till there, though the lingering scent of Polo Blue had disappeared.

No words were said. I handed the sweater to Margarita. She hugged it to her.

"Wait. Before you go, Mary Beth, I want to give you

something, too." Margarita fumbled around in her purse and came up with a key. Neither of us had to ask. The key was unquestionably another key to the Loomis Hall corridor.

"Where did this come from, Margarita?"

"Why, from Les, of course. I don't need it any longer. I won't be dropping into his office any more, will I?"

What could I do? I smiled sympathetically, took the key, said thanks, and left.

When Tony and I counted keys later, he pointed out that if Margarita's touch of the occult hadn't initiated a panic attack, I might have learned something. Margarita had talked a little more about how influenced Les was by Stew. She said that Les thought his dissertation was going to lead him to great things.

"How could it?" I asked Tony. "Stew not only teaches colonialism. He thinks he owns it. He wouldn't share his field with Les."

"How could Les think it would lead to 'great things'?" Tony asked, ignoring the fact I had just asked the same question. "Not if 'great things' has anything to do with income," he replied to himself. "George Herbert said it in 1630 and you know it's still true today, 'The love of money and the love of learning rarely meet.' Maybe we should find and read Stew's original dissertation, Mary Best. Then we'd know."

"Maybe we should ask Stew for a précis, Tony. I'm not going to read 250 pages about *The Raj Response to Comparative Classics* or anything else. Anyway it's going to boil down to colonialism and people of color. You know, as in Les's work of *Black vs. White.*"

Tony pushed the subject away with a negative shake of his head. "Better than this dissertation stuff, Mary Beth, is that Margarita got more and more confidential and blushingly confided in me that Charlie, yes, your friend Charlie, had made a pass at her. She said that it was such an overt pass that she had thought of registering it as sexual harassment, but Les talked her out of it."

"Boy. Did we let Charlie con us. And he even told us about the College's zero tolerance in regard to him and sexual harassment."

"What if Les used Margarita's information to blackmail Charlie?" Tony suggested. "I wouldn't put it past him."

"You're right, Tony. Now take it to the next step. You spent two years in Princeton as an architect for artificial intelligence. Put it to use on the unsub's . . . "

"The what?" Tony stopped me in the midst of my mixing computer and detective metaphors.

"Unsub, unknown subject or perp. I'm beginning to talk the talk. Put your artificial intelligence skills to use on the unsub's real intelligence. Imagine some virtual corridors that lead to the motive of the person who killed Les and Krypto. Isn't that what you do when you're not repairing bicycles or writing your book? And I don't see how anyone's dissertation could fit in."

"It might explain why Stew and Les were so close. We have to find out what Les's connection was with each member of your department. I think Charlie hardly knew he was there, but some of the others seemed to have had complicated relationships with him."

"You do it. I've got to run. I have to get back to class. I gave my kids a journal writing assignment, but it can't go on forever. Just wanted a five-minute break to talk with you, hon. You've always been my base, but right now I need you even more; I think I'd be as manic as everyone else around here without you. At least Margarita is still concerned about Les. Has everyone else forgotten about him? We'll see. Meet you at lunch with The Next Suspect."

Trying to break down the psychological barriers that the faculty lunchroom or a campus hangout would impose, we had invited Gary to my house. Punctually at 12 noon he pounded on the door and gave us a perfunctory (translation, what's this all about?) greeting. Seeing the floor covered with all of my research materials by authors who were old friends to him did the trick. He mellowed out enough to sit in my only comfortable chair, sip a beer, and watch me show off my cooking skills which consisted of moving from the refrigerator to the table the garden of salads I had culled from all of the delis and supermarkets in town: chicken salad, tuna salad, potato salad, mushroom and artichokes, asparagus salad, ham salad, macaroni salad, various suspiciously similar concoctions labeled Greek pasta salad (with feta cheese), Italian pasta salad (with parmesan) and French pasta salad (with brie). "Wow, Mary Beth," our guest exclaimed, "you must have cornered the Midfield lunch market, lock, stock, bagel and schmear."

'Schmear' in Midfield? I winced. Was Gary an 'oyster,' one who sprinkles his conversations with Yiddishisms? Or was it only in front of me? Or was I again getting a tad paranoid?

I might have gone a little over the top for a casual lunch, but Gary already had me so nervous. I wasn't going to give him an excuse to yell at me this time because I didn't have the one item he wanted! So I put tea in the teapot, bread in the breadbasket-after unobtrusively dusting off the few rolls that had fallen on the floor-and the scene was set. Pleased with myself for once, I helped Tony and Gary fill their plates.

But a knock that Tony and I hadn't scripted changed my smugness to chagrin. We had spent too much time concocting questions and subtle probings of Gary, planning to watch out for his tell-tale eye blinks and finger twistings to be distracted by a chatty neighbor wanting to borrow the proverbial cup of sugar. I had to answer the door. Just call me surprised. "Seth, what are you doing here?" is perhaps not the most polite way to greet a guest, but Seth didn't seem to mind.

"Heard you three were having lunch together, so I thought I'd stop by and make it a party."

"What?" Self-restraint kept me from asking if we were acting out some kind of a thriller with spies spying on the spy.

"I wasn't investigating when I called the English department secretary. I just phoned to set up an appointment and Ms. Wallace told me where you all were," was Seth's satisfactory explanation.

"Looks pretty good, Mary Beth," he nodded in the general direction of the table. "How you doing, Gary? What've you been up to the last couple of days?"

"You know darn well what I've been up to, Detective Yoder." He waved away Seth's attempt at a "Just-Call-Me" interruption and responded to that unstated correction.

"I'll call you whatever I want to. It wouldn't take much detecting on your part to guess I've been searching for proof of my alibi. I know I was at the Buck, buck-eled in, so to speak. See, contrary to what I know is popular opinion; I do have a sense of humor. I was working in a computer carrel when Les was murdered. Those librarians think I'm right, but they're too damn goody-goody to swear to something they just 'think' is right. I have my computer check-out card around some place. I keep all records. Don't worry, I'll find it. I would have found it by now if you and your local Keystone cops hadn't messed up my office so much.

"I am trying to help. I'm trying to give you pertinent information right now. You should know that only five of us are permitted to have keys to the Loomis Hall corridor. Roger, Charlie, Stew, Mary Beth, and I are the only ones allowed the key. Since I am the one who made that rule for security reasons, I could use my own discretion about breaking it. Of course, I had a copy made for my friend Victoria." Tony and I didn't dare look at each other, but instead kept our eyes on Gary who was still reciting his monologue.

"The second thing you should know is that I didn't like Les. He managed to be furtive and smug at the same time. Believe me, 'furtive' and 'smug' are euphemisms for what I really think. Les is the kind of a guy who ordered that expensive 'purple and white/fight, fight' Cannondale bike everyone's talking about, and probably never intended to pay for it. But I don't like murders in my office either. So, while going through files looking for my Buckeye receipt, I've also kept an eye open to see if I had anything that might pertain to your investigation, Mr. Detective Yoder.

"I did come up with the copy of one reference letter that Les asked me to write for him. I write basically the same letter for every student who asks for one. It's a neat, time-saving academic trick I've developed. The students are always thrilled. They don't realize that the glowing terms I show them are just generalizations: 'innovative mind but not a boat rocker' or 'outstanding teaching assistant' could mean anything. After the student leaves and before I mail the approved letter, I always add a personal note, 'call me.' If anyone calls," Gary had the nerve to chuckle, "I tell him the real truth."

In an acute state of disbelief, I thought of all the false hopes raised, the job application letters not answered, the interviews not granted because of Gary's deceitfulness. With that kind of power he wouldn't ever have to physically kill anyone, or would he?

Seth ignored the emotional tenseness and kept to the detecting business, demonstrating again the difference between an amateur (me) and a professional (him); not that either of us ever had any doubts. "A less than glowing reference letter in today's job market might give Les cause to throttle you, Gary, but it doesn't help our investigation. I know that there was bad blood between you two. I've heard of the fist fight that took place a couple of weeks ago."

Gary bristled, "Can you imagine that kid attacking me? Me?"

"Well, asking anyone to unknowingly conduct interviews for his own job would not exactly endear you to an employee, but no matter where I take that exploration, it doesn't make you Mr. Number One suspect."

"Please don't tell me that the Sheriff's Department is innocent in the field of office politics. That's all that it was. Les shouldn't have been so shocked. So I was using him, he thought in a rather nasty way. If he wanted to play with the big boys . . . ."

"We don't need to hear your management philosophy spelled out, Gary. It's clear that the fight and the reasons behind it don't give you motivation to kill Les, rather the other way around. No need to worry. I think as we work through this investigation, you and I will understand each other completely."

"I doubt that," was Gary's rejoinder.

Rising above the dig, Seth continued. "So, let's look at what we do have. Mary Beth talked to me once about social anthropology. Well, detecting work is something like that or maybe digging in the body for clues is more like archeology, one or the other. We're looking for specific finds. What we've finished doing is sifting through the first layer, that's fingerprints. We've had excellent help from Columbus's Automatic Fingerprint Identification System. AFIS is a superior computerized system and it gave us zilch. The corkscrew was wiped clean and the paper weight had everyone's fingerprints on it."

Yes, mine, too, I thought. Been there. Done that.

While I was nervously turning that paperweight again in my mind, Seth had continued, ". . . seriously digging in deeper levels, including blood work. We'll have some DNA results Monday. By the way, we've confirmed that the corkscrew and paperweight found at the scene were definitely yours, Gary."

"I'm sure of it," Gary cut off Seth's detailed forensic explanation. "The paperweight's an antique. And whoever those people are who said they have a corkscrew just like the one in that dog, don't. They have cheap imitations. Mine is German, hand finished and precision made of 100% high-carbon, finest grade stainless steel." Was Gary giving a commercial for bottle openers? Or just being carried away by his own rhetoric? He continued, "The curved handle of olive wood and brushed steel fits the hand perfectly."

He looked up, startled at the implications of what he had said. "Not my hand. At least, not then. But that forged-steel screw could obviously open or pull out an artery as easily as it could open a bottle and pull out a cork. Probably with the same soft plunk, too."

Without a break, seamlessly, as we say in the English department, Gary continued his concentrated reading of the book titles that surrounded him while enjoying assorted salads.

Not one of us could say a word. Rolled eyes were our only signal to each other. Gary's "soft plunk" of the artery had been the final words in conversation stoppers.

Would this lunch never be over? I couldn't even lie about having a Thursday, 1 o'clock class. Gary knew my schedule.

I directed a plea-for-help look to Tony with the subterfuge of turning my back to refill his plate. By the third time I refilled it with tuna salad (and Tony knows that I know he hates tuna salad), Tony caught on. "Have to change into my work clothes and get back to the shop, Mary Beth. Hate to break this up, but as Voltaire said, 'Work helps to preserve us from great evils.' And," he whispered as he walked out of the door, "our luncheon is surely what he must have had in mind!"

Chapter Sixteen

"Should I, after tea and cakes and ices,
Have the strength to force the moment to its crisis?"

The Love Song of J. Alfred Prufrock, T. S. Eliot

❧

Tea time with Roger wasn't until the following day, thank goodness. I do have classes to teach. Persuading undergraduates to see the structural similarity between Forster's straight and homosexual short stories, "The Eternal Moment" and "The Other Boat," isn't difficult. It is difficult, however, and takes more planning to get them to think that these structures could carry meaning, then to motivate them to search for sexual similarities that are otherwise disguised in the 'straight' story. Structuralism is out of style today in the field of Literary Criticism, but I want my students to understand that the study of structure is still a productive tool to use in uncovering the author's meanings. The time spent playing even amateur detective was beginning to erode preparation hours needed for effective teaching.

Students and faculty celebrate T.G.I.F. each week at the two bars in town strategically placed the shortest possible legal walking distance from campus. But as befits British Lit. Profs, also for the sake of privacy, Roger and I planned to meet at 5 p.m. to drink tea, not beer. We met where everyone meets on campus-at the Clock Tower. The red brick tower was donated to the school in 1912 by Professor Everett Ellsworth, who had been President and re-vitalizer of the college. It has become a symbol of Midfield, town and campus, immortalized as one of the towers on the infamous McCollege T-shirts.

Leaving campus together, we took advantage of the beautiful autumn day to stroll just beyond bar territory to our date with Tony at the Midfield Motor Inn. It's not much of a choice to walk to the inn-Midfield doesn't have any public transportation, and Roger's properly aged Volvo in Faculty Parking was just as long a walk away as the Midfield Motor Inn's restaurant-cum-tea shop would be, but in the opposite direction. Tea at the Mid doesn't have quite the panache of tea at Simpsons' on the Strand, though by now, even the Mid offers an assortment of teas-all in tea bags, of course. Since much of academic life is pretense anyway, we easily imagined we were having a proper British tea.

Our happy game was aided by Tony's arrival on his totally black Paramount bicycle with those recycled

Campognola parts. Tony's striped scarf was picturesquely blowing behind him. Could his Oakley M Frames, Lance Armstrong edition, have been just too cool? Tony loped in through the door and joined us in a booth. We ordered "tea and cakes and ices," but the teatime mood didn't last long at all. Instead of demonstrating British restraint, as soon as we were served, Roger took a few sips of tea, put it down, and blurted, "I have the best motive."

"What?" even unflappable Tony was taken by surprise.

But I was sitting next to Roger and could see the nervous tremors of his leg. I swear I could feel the table vibrating. Something was up. At the least, he needed to see a therapist about habit management.

"Look, I know you two are helping Detective Yoder with the Les case. Everyone knows it. I don't presume it was even supposed to be any kind of a secret. How could it be with your calling everyone in the department for these little tete a têtes? We do compare notes, you know," he added getting more emotional with each sentence.

"I'm sure we all want to help," I replied somewhat inanely, mainly trying to calm him down before decibel and emotive rating were beyond control. "Tony and I have mentioned to Seth Yoder that we would run some first-round interviews for him."

Roger's tremors were intensifying to the point where I wasn't the only one who noticed. "What's with the speeded-up personal pedal cadence?" Tony whispered. He didn't have to talk in bike talk. Roger didn't hear the remark; he was concentrating. I had to, too.

A few minutes ago Roger had been shouting; now he was speaking so lowly and intently that it was difficult to understand him. "I'm glad it's you, Mary Beth. You're O.K. too, Tony, but I mean it's easier to talk with Mary Beth-as-academician. You'll have to tell me how to explain this to Yoder. It's all about internal standards. I'm not sure he'll understand."

"Explain what?" I took some quick swallows of my tea, happy that I had ordered black, strong Irish breakfast tea instead of a caffeine free or one of those herbal varieties. I couldn't afford to be relaxed.

"You know how I've been begging to be allowed to vote in the department? To get back in so I could vote? All of that was just to help Les get his doctorate and immediately find a tenure track job here at Midfield," Roger said, his eyes asking me for an understanding that wasn't forthcoming since I still had no idea what his problem was.

"So where's a murder motive there?" Tony blurted. "Unless it's that you're practically killing the guy with kindness. Plus, I understand at times," and he looked at me though his words were still directed to Roger, "you seem to be sacrificing your own reputation by almost begging to be allowed to help Les."

Roger shrugged, "You don't think I was doing it because I liked or admired Les, do you? Believe me I didn't. I don't. He had a hold over me. He needed a couple of credits to finish his degree at Ohio State. The university would accept an independent study project with me, so we signed a three-way contract. I gave him a one-semester tutorial. That's all he needed to make up his missing two credits. And that was that, I thought. But I had forgotten a department requirement for a term paper, so had to insert it in the contract after it was signed and filed. I'll admit I did it-without telling him. This might not sound like a heinous crime to the non-academic, but Mary Beth, you understand how illegally I acted."

Did I! Professors have been dethroned and defrocked for lesser crimes than this one. The trust between student and faculty member is held sacred in every university. Professional journals have been full of recent cases of an Adjunct Prof. in Indiana and a Professor with Endowed Chair in Vermont who betrayed that faith. The cases also show how tenuous a hold professors have on their jobs. I sat thinking about Roger's statement for a while. Were we finally being confronted with a clue?

Roger was continuing, "During our last tutorial week, I mentioned to Les that he had to write a paper. He could have easily brought me up for a hearing on disciplinary charges for unilaterally ratifying a class requirement addendum to a contract. I never would have gotten back in the department after that and I sure wouldn't have advanced in administration."

"Roger, are you going a long way around the barn to tell us that Les was blackmailing you?"

"Well, if you want to put it plainly. Yes. At first it was

for small ransoms, small victories to show he had power. He wanted a key to the Loomis corridor. I wouldn't have even given that to him if he hadn't threatened to tell all to the Dean of Faculty. But then he upped his requests. He wanted me to vote to have him hired for a tenure-track position."

Roger stiffened. "So I did have a motive. But really I was in my office in the Ad. Building until just before we were supposed to have our Monday department meeting. Someone must have seen me, the administrative secretary for sure. Mary Beth, can you explain all of this to the sheriff? He'll never understand about contracts and term papers and how important they can be."

Tony hmmmed. "As Henry David Thoreau said back in the 19th century, 'some circumstantial evidence is very strong, as when you find a trout in the milk.' Most people would think that your motive is that trout, Roger, but in this case I believe you. I mean that both ways. I certainly believe your devious motive. But I also believe that you did not kill Les. He might have been blackmailing you, but you aren't one to use the direct approach to problem solving!"

Did Roger realize that Tony was insulting him even as he was excusing him? Maybe, because with Tony's last remark Roger left our tea party with some mumbling about getting home to make dinner; it was his night to cook.

"That explains the expensive Cannondale," Tony said the minute Roger went out the door. " . . . especially if Les was blackmailing Charlie, too. No wonder he got along so well on a part-timer's pay."

Tony and I exchanged glances and each ordered another cup of tea, this time green with ginseng, hoping that it might have some mystical powers. We were again coming to the point where we needed all the extra help we could get.

"Mary Beth, I never realized how hard detecting is. We've met with almost all of the suspects and I still don't have any ideas! First we had no motives. Now we have too many! What would real detectives do? Maybe we should forget about people, except for tomorrow night's supper with Stew and Seth, and take a much closer look at the real clues from the murder scene. We're spending too much time on non-clues, like the keys. I'm going back to my digs now and try to think through the evidence scientifically."

I started to remind Tony that we had a Sunday breakfast with Purley, too, but I saw that preoccupied look and noticed that as he was speaking to me, his fingers were sorting through his color coded graphing pens always at the ready in his geeky engineer's pocket protector.

The last words I could hear before the door banged behind him were, "Maybe I can make a simple table of what we know, starting with Charlie's hating dogs."

Chapter Seventeen

*"It is no easy task to pick one's way from truth to truth
through besetting errors."*

Collected works, Peter Mere Latham, 1789-1875

❧

F.Y.I., M.B.
It's as easy as a.b.c.d.
(A. BARTLETT'S CLUE DIRECTORY)
Mary Beth, see two attached pages.

Clues as I See Them

Facts	Comments/Questions
Blood, plenty of it	My jeans, MB's briefcase, anyone else's? Yes, saw some stacked in Gary's office
Blood tests DNA results due Monday	Can we see results?
Fingerprints	Seems a dead end: too many or not enough
Paperweight. Dead-end for fingerprints. Too many. Les struck with it, but not the murder weapon	Why used? To disguise real cause of death?
Corkscrew. Murder weapon for Krypto	Another fingerprint dead end. Wiped clean. Real question here is why was Krypto killed? What kind of a nut murders a dog? (Tony-make 2nd list for suspects)
Cork from red wine in waste basket Some bottlers' markings	Not usable for fingerprints - B.C.I. (Tony-Find someone who knows something about corks.) Can we learn anything at all from cork? Some people sniff cork. Purley says crystals on cork indicate better wine. Lure for Les?
Wine bottle, glasses. gone	Probably paper cups.
	What was murder weapon?

Suspects as I See Them

Facts/Names	Comments/Questions
Eliminated	
1. Margarita Berenguer 2. Curley Purley	Seriously in love with Les, the one person genuinely in mourning. Substantiated alibi of conference, giving paper at American Chem. Society. Besides, our friend!
Suspicious	
1. Gary Hake	Everyone wants him to be the guilty one. Corkscrew, paperweight, and office (scene of the crime) are his. Says he was in library. Librarians aren't sure. Says he can prove it.
2. Roger Christian	Has motive, being blackmailed by Les. Says alibi is he was in his office. Says administrative secretary must have seen him. Not confirmed.
3. Stew Jones	Dinner with him and Seth tomorrow. For sure he'll come up with amusing alibi. Not so sure I can take much more of him.
4. Charlie Volstadt	Hates dogs. Could this be a motive for killing Krypto? Says alibi is he was in bed. No witnesses. Being blackmailed by Les?

Chapter Eighteen

"How much better is thy love than wine!"

Song of Solomon

"Why not have both?"

Tony Bartlett

❧

The charts were hand delivered by my favorite delivery man early Saturday morning.

"They're great, Tony. I wish I could put my thoughts in this kind of order.

"'Oh! Blessed rage for order . . .' That's from one of your literary buddies, Mary Babe. Wallace Stevens. Right now I've got enough order for both of us. The charts are nothing. I've got more arranged than a few clues and suspects."

"What're you talking about, Hon?"

"I'm talking about us. Enough of this crime solving.

Enough of grading student essays, responding to love-sick journal entries."

"I never should have told you about Amos, Tony."

"Enough of what we've been going through this week. We're taking this beautiful Saturday off. We don't have to be back until dinner with Seth and Co. Right? Look at this, Mary Best."

I tried to look, but Tony's waving arm presented difficulties. "I can see you're fanning us with a paperback, Tony. Is it called Bike Trails?"

"Better than Bike Trails, Mary Beth, it's Bike Trails of Ohio. It not only describes city park trails and old canal trails, but trails that lead to 42 Ohio wineries. The book is divided into five geographical sections and shows six wineries near us in the section called Ohio Heartland. One winery is just a few miles outside of Midfield. We'll have a few hills, but they're nothing, even though tourist brochures label this part of Ohio 'Little Switzerland.' Don't worry. You won't have to play Heidi. This isn't Alpine country. We're not even in the foothills. Do you think you're good for an hour's easy biking?"

"Sure I am, Tony, if I can use any of my swimming muscles. This should be good practice for the wine trip we talked about taking during Spring Break, though I'm not sure I can handle a wine trail of ten wineries around Lake Erie. The biking along with all of that wine tasting might be a little too much. Maybe we should wait and go on Amos's Great Ohio Alpaca Tour next September.

"Just kidding. What do I have to bring for our practice

run?"

"Nothing, Mary Beth. I really have planned a day trip for us. All you have to do is to put on some sun screen. Take your sunglasses and helmet. Your phone for emergencies."

I followed Tony's instructions, adding a windbreaker. Even on a beautiful autumn day, the warning of an Ohio winter was an undercurrent in the air.

"The Wine Cellar at Midfield Crick has everything we'll need." Tony explained as he checked the air in my tires. "If this works out, I think we'll take the Heritage wine trail instead of the Lake Erie one. It's about a half a dozen wineries right here in the Heartland."

We closed the door behind us and walked our bikes down the path to the sidewalk. My patriotic Raleigh and Tony's cool, black Paramount make an odd couple. Hmmm. A metaphor for Tony and me?

We headed out of town, passing the bowling alley that marks the city limits. It's much more of a landmark than the nearby official, newly painted sign, "Welcome to Midfield-Gateway to the Midwest." Then we peddled past Amos's alpaca ranch where I recognized a few of the pet inhabitants.

I concentrated on avoiding the minimal traffic and trying to hear Tony who was shouting the day's plans at me. "I've called ahead. We'll join a wine tour that sounds like fun. We can have a late lunch right on the premises and be home in plenty of time to take a nap or whatever," (significant pause!) "and still be ready for Seth and Stew. The little old winemaker barbeques outside whenever the weather permits and it sure permits today. Anyway they have a market there. We can make a picnic. Let's roll, Mary Babe. We need this time out."

It was a beautiful day. The sun was shining. Leaves were turning to those wonderful reds and golds of Ohio forests. Purple vetch and autumnal wild flowers, planted by the Keep Ohio Beautiful Committee, outlined the roads. But even though we were carefully shun-piking, I wasn't an experienced enough biker to take my eyes off of the path ahead of me and enjoy the scenery.

I didn't miss too much because Tony carried on a running description of every hay stack we passed, though most of them were the more modern hay rolls. What I could see of them looked as if someone had spilled a package of shredded wheat across the fields. I did much better a half hour later when we turned on to the Old County Route 1. We entered a slightly kitschy commercial area, ready for Amish tour buses. Tony said, "We're almost there, Mary Babe. As soon as we pass the Word of Life Fellowship on the left and the Grand Champion Cheese and Lace Curtain Shop-honest!-on the right, you'll see the Marketplatz. The winery is just behind it."

We pulled in and parked our bikes in the rack next to an Amish buggy. The buggy was for atmosphere. You don't find many Amish on a wine tour! We stretched and looked around. A group of about 15 senior citizens were disembarking from a mini-bus and standing in clumps in the courtyard, some investigating the Amish buggy, some looking longingly at the stop they hadn't made at the Champion Cheese and Lace Curtain Shop. Next trip . . .

The little old winemaker who turned out to be in his 40s, taller than Tony, and a Harrison Ford look-alike came out of the market and blew a small silver whistle to summon the meandering group. A small silver whistle? He told us later that some friends from Midfield Campus College had given it to him. President Bender was right. Those whistles do come in handy.

Our leader introduced himself: Duke Cherkowksi, owner, manager, and winemaker for the Wine Cellar at Midfield Crick. He welcomed everyone and with a slow wink at me explained that two people from neighboring, prestigious Midfield Campus College would be joining the group. "That's us," Tony nudged.

"The tour proper will take about 20 minutes," Duke explained. "You can ask questions as we go along. And you'll be happy to know-it makes me happy, too-that your Cincinnati tour company has allowed you plenty of time to shop at the Marketplatz before getting back on the bus. This wine cellar has been in business 26 years. We know what we're doing. We do it well. If you do enough wine tasting afterwards, I'm sure you'll agree with me." This well rehearsed remark was greeted with appreciative giggles. "We buy grapes from 30 different Ohio vineyards that grow the fruit according to my specifications. With those grapes we produce 130,000 gallons of wine a year."

He kept us standing in the courtyard while he showed

us where the hand-picked grapes were tumbled into the hopper and where their skins were split in the crushing station. The outdoor lecture ended with a brief description of the way white, red, and rose wines were processed. Then we moved into the large winery buildings that were surprisingly full of state-of-the-art machinery and large oak barrels.

Duke started to tell us how he makes champagne, demonstrating the 1/8 of a turn daily riddling by turning the racks as he was speaking. Pointing to me, he asked if anyone in the group would like to help. With that slight change of focus, Duke revolved the angled bottles 1/8th of a turn too far and, unbelievably, 500 bottles full of champagne fell to the cement floor. I had never realized I could be that distracting! The accident sounded like small bombs going off in a battle zone: the bottles breaking, the explosion of 500 champagne corks, the screams (most of them were with delight) of the tourists. Duke blew his silver whistle, "This is not the way we usually make champagne," he grinned. A quick hand signal to the department manager started the clean-up process, while Duke led us to the next room and smoothly went on with the tour. He was cool. No one else saw him give me another of those slow winks of his.

After the tour, the group went into the Marketplatz for some frantic shopping and just as frantic wine tasting. Twenty minutes of lecturing and the excitement of the champagne blow-up had made our fellow tourists thirsty.

Duke followed us in and said to me, "State law requires that I charge you, but I'd like you to try some of my private

stock, Professor. You, too, Tony."

"We're both driving," we answered in chorus.

Duke escorted us back into the winery where he took a wine thief to borrow samples from three different barrels. "Because you're 'driving,' I'll give you small samples of red wines now. Maybe you'll come back some other time, Professor, for a full tasting."

Tony and I tried two cabernets and a rather bland merlot. I could taste such distinct after-flavors of chocolate in one sample and some berry in another that I asked Duke if he added anything to the grapes. "No," he said, "it's the kind of grape and especially the kind of wooden barrel that's used. We hold the wines one to four years. The ones you're tasting are older. That affects the taste too. We employ no additives whatsoever. But it's funny that you should ask. One of your colleagues from the College was here about a month ago asking about additives in our wines too. More were here last week and gave me this whistle. You guys going to start a new major? I'll be glad to be a guest lecturer."

We laughed off the suggestion, thanked Duke, and wandered around the grounds for a while. Instead of waiting for his barbeque, we bought some Ohio bread, cheeses, and cold sausages in the Marketplatz and had a private picnic outside in the gazebo provided for that purpose.

It was a perfect afternoon, but if we were going to get home in time to dress to go out with Stew and Seth, we had to start peddling back to campus.

"I hate to leave, Hon. It's been such a great day," I said

as we mounted our bikes again. We'd been biking for just a few minutes when my cell phone rang. As I picked it up, Tony rode past me shouting into the wind and, through the phone, into my ear, "I am drunken, but not with wine. Happiness is the rarest vintage."

A for subject matter; C for twisting quotes from the Bible and L. P. Smith together as one. Final grade A+. My Tony.

Chapter Nineteen

"Let Hercules himself do what he may/The cat will mew and dog will have his day."

Hamlet V, 1600-1601 Shakespeare

❧

That last-minute phone call from Seth changed our big Saturday night out restauranting with him and Stew to the most informal locale of his downtown office. Seth had found Thursday's at-home lunch with Gary profitable to his understanding of the case. He did not want to miss out on the chance to learn more during the semi-social Saturday night dinner we had planned with Stew. But last minute necessary paper work complicated by red tape meant he didn't have the time or inclination for a Saturday night out at a noisy, crowded local bar-cum-dining spot. So, since Seth couldn't come to a restaurant, it followed that we should come to his office, a Midfield application of Mohammed and the mountain.

Seth's office has that worked-in look that keeps his usual interviews with townies or students from being too threatening. But as a place to dine? Wow. Seth's vintage wooden desk takes up the biggest portion of the room, the four chairs (two were garage-sale bridge chairs borrowed for the occasion) take up almost as much space. All together, the furniture and filing cabinet created an uncomfortably intimate area for the four of us to eat and talk. Where in the world had he put all of the papers that cluttered his desk the last time I was here? The desk was now our table, not spotless, it would take a good sanding and re-finishing job for that, but more than adequate for a take-out picnic. "Don't worry about what we'll eat. I'll order in some Chinese," Seth had said on the phone. And sure enough, just a few minutes after we arrived, so did Su Ming balancing white cardboard cartons full of everything on the menu from his restaurant, appropriately named "Su Ming's."

"I didn't know what anyone liked," Seth explained the lavish (well, lavish for the occasion) display.

Su Ming set the cartons down on the table, saw me, and said, "Oh, Dr. Goldberg, ma'am," (ma'am?) "my daughter Alice really likes your class in freshman composition." Su and I had been friends since I ordered Tony's birthday cake from his bakery annex. Su reinterpreted the "Mazel Tov" I had asked to be written on the cake to the more familiar (to him) "Mazel Tong"! Who could resist? We laughed over our cultural differences and struck up a friendship.

"Alice is a good student, Mr. Ming," I was fortunate

enough to be able to reply. "She is at the top of the class."
Ming smiled at the answer he, as proud father, expected. In
return, he suggested that for best feng shui results, I should
move my chair away from the door.

Move my chair? I smiled. Ming looked around at the
size of the room and smiled too, admitting there was little
room to maneuver. Then he handed me a plastic package
of fortune cookies. "Try one of these now, Professor. I had
them made especially for my campus catering service to
controversial meetings. This might be one if you can't
rearrange the chairs." He waited expectantly while I broke
open the cookie and burst out laughing as I read,

> *"There's no fuming*
> *When you eat Su Ming."*

When Ming left, nodding and beaming over my eval-
uation of Alice and appreciation of his self-deprecating
humor, we dug into our luke-warm egg rolls and sweet and
sour pork strips. From the bottom of the bags I distributed
condiments, paper napkins, and those wooden chopsticks
that come in inseparable pairs—woman's role. Even here!
Even now! Even in the middle of an investigative discussion.

"So, how far have we gotten in solving Les's murder?"
Seth's sudden question urged us back immediately to the
subject we had convened to discuss. He knew darn well
that each one of us wanted to ask our own version of that
same question. Each one of us wanted an answer.

"I knew we weren't meeting here to discuss my team-teaching with Mary Beth next semester," Stew started.

He was quick to elaborate. "We usually do our 'building of teaching communities' on campus. So, what are the four of us doing here? Starting the 'building of investigative communities'?"

"And what about Krypto?" he added, adeptly chop-sticking fried rice direct from the carton to his mouth.

"Yep, too bad she's not still around to help solve the crime. Border collies have such good scenting ability that they can find sheep in snow banks. Maybe she could have found our murderer for us," Seth answered.

Stew leaned forward to say something. Expecting a Stew-ism, I fixed my mouth in a smile. But Stew just wanted to show off more canine expertise, "I'll bet she could have. She was very smart. Border collies are supposed to be smarter than their masters, the smartest of all breeds, and she was especially sharp. I saw on the Internet that Border collies can learn to understand human speech. She really could have pointed to the murderer."

Tony, our major collector of trivia, joined in to ask if anyone had read the news article about the Geese Police. "They're Border collies that help people get rid of those messy Canada geese. In New Jersey, they've even got deputy dogs. And with fancier badges than you sport, Seth. Gonna put you out of business."

Tony turned serious, "'Caveat canem' as the old Latin proverb has it. 'Beware of the dog.'"

"Not any more," Stew said unable to resist a pun.

"She's not going to tell tales out of school now-get it?"

Seth was busy with his chopsticks, doodling pictures of one box after the other in his left over soy sauce. I guess our chitchat was vapid enough to make the truly responsible person among us a tad impatient. Pointing the chopsticks at his drawings, he blurted out, "I don't care if you think in the box or out of the box, but think about this case for a while instead of the qualifications for the Kensington dog show.

"My questioning you might seem abrupt, Stew, but we aren't here to trump each other's doggy puns. We are talking about a murder or murders, and we haven't heard from your corner. Where were you mid-afternoon Monday?"

"I was home, Seth. I have an hour or so between my last Monday class and the regular faculty meeting so I almost always go home to check with my wife. Have you met Sally? Anyway I go home then because I know I won't be home until late. Depending on who is speaking, those meetings can be interminable. Of course, if I'm the one doing most of the talking, I find them exquisitely engrossing."

"Was Sally home with you this past Monday?"

"Of course. She'll remember because she had some new Internet jokes that she thought I might like to add to my repertoire."

Was this true? Were there two of them? I wondered about this odd joke collecting couple, keeping what I think was a straight face, an intent gaze.

"Well, that's easy to check on," Seth replied. "Do you mind if I call Sally right now?"

"Be my guest."

"Then excuse me a minute," said Seth. He pushed back his chair.

Before he had enough leg room to stand, Stew leaped up. "Wait. Excuse me a minute. Maybe I do have something pertinent to say. This is the time for a confession."

What? Tony and I exchanged 'can-you-believe-this?' glances.

Stew gained momentum. "Sally will tell you, so you should hear it first from me. Sally has a key to the corridor."

Well, this kind of confession we'd heard before. We could accept this, I thought.

"It made our lives simpler when she had access to the corridor and my office," Stew explained. "If I was out of town at a conference and forgot a paper, which has happened, she could retrieve it and fax it to me."

"Everyone's a suspect," Seth grumbled as he left for a more private office to place his call. Stew sat down deflated. The three of us adjusted our chairs to take up the space he had vacated. We needed to expand our legs and lungs and breathe a little. Having run out of things to say to each other, we busied ourselves by playing with cold rice and congealed plum sauce. What if Stew's 'confession' was made to distract us? What if his alibi didn't hold? What if we were sharing chow mein with a murderer, though I couldn't believe that. We all avoided eye contact. The silence had passed being awkward. I was beginning to feel the stress of social responsibility to the point of almost ask-

ing Stew if he had heard any good ones lately when Seth came back in to say to Stew in a tone that included all of us, "Sally says that she saw you come home before 3 p.m. and leave just before 5 p.m., around the time you usually leave for faculty meetings. Sounds good to me."

"Me, too," Stew replied. We all relaxed.

Tony charged in, taking the conversation by the handlebars, so to speak, "Let's stay in the box, Seth, until we get a few more questions answered. Can you tell us what the results of the blood test were?"

"Disappointing."

"What does that mean?"

"No matches with Les's blood, except on your jeans, Tony. Someone was carefully clean Monday afternoon. We thought we had one more blood sample on a briefcase, but no go, no match."

Tap. Tap. Tap. Came the repeated response from Tony's seat.

"What's with the chop sticks, Tony?"

"Look, Seth, I'm an engineer and a quotation collector. I don't look at things the same way a trained detective or professors do." He turned to me, "After I constructed those two charts, Mary Beth, I stared at them for a while until the one with the list of suspects began to take shape. A quotation came to me. You know that one by DeQuincey, 'if once a man indulges himself in murder, very soon he comes to think little of robbing, and from robbing he comes next to drinking and Sabbath-breaking, and from that to incivility and procrastination'? Well, look at this chart and think about it."

Those cartoon light bulbs started to go off in my head. "Right again, Tony, my dear quotation master, we have the drinker, Charlie Volstadt. We have Roger Christian, a guy who delights in Sabbath-breaking. There's incivility, for sure, with Gary. And as for you, Stew, you have to admit procrastination is your middle name, also your destiny and salvation. It's mine, too."

"I can play that game too," Seth jumped in. "All we need now is someone who is guilty of robbery. I know no money is involved, but it just might be robbery of a good name or, hey, of intellectual property. Good out-of-the-box thinking, Tony."

"We're on a roll. I email the American Intellectual Property Law Association regularly for pro bono help with the use of my own name for my *Bartlett's Better Book of Quotations*. I'll bet we could get some help from them. They'd answer our questions."

"Whoa. What are our questions?"

Stew was getting red, and it wasn't from additives. Seth had told Su Ming to leave out the MSG.

"Yes, 'what are your questions?' You're getting way off the subject, and I have other things to do. I'm leaving this party. Ahem," he vocally pointed, "you're as *Clueless* as *Emma*." Stew stood up after giving us his parting shot, somewhat spoiling the effect by waiting long enough to see that I appreciated his Jane Austen literary allusion.

"What's with him?" I asked my fellow players. "He didn't even wait to read his fortune cookie."

Chapter Twenty

"And seek for truth in the groves of Academe."

Epistles, book 2, 14 b.c.

❧

Sunday morning Tony and I got up early after an active night that had pulled the sheets off of the bed. I wonder if anyone manufactures heat-resistant sheets! Of course, before we could leave, Tony had to strip and remake the bed, hospital corners and all. So we had time for coffee only before meandering over to mid-America's idea of a deli, Kroger's. We picked up hot bagels there for our Sunday brunch with Curley and Janet Purlis. I purposefully wore one of Janet's stunning chunky, ethnic looking, pieces of jewelry. She's her own best model for her work, but she gave me this piece as a gift when we first hit it off. It's so effective and flattering, giving me a lot of cultural and arty gravitas, that I've bought a necklace and some earrings from her since then. I thought she might notice that I was the second best model!

More proof of friends' thinking alike, Janet was walking up to her door at the same time we were and toting the same size Kroger's bag with one hand. Only as she walked, she kicked aside some of the usual children's detritus that lined the driveway. We'd been preoccupied with not tripping over it.

"Hey, Nick and Nora," she called between sips of water from a bottle she precariously balanced. "Did we cross signals? Did we both stop for hot bagels? Not a problem. I'll freeze some and have you over for a real brunch once this terrible murder is solved. Come on in. Curt's busy assembling orange juice and coffee."

"Thanks, Janet, it's always fun being here," I replied, sniffing the bacon-scented air as Tony and I split to avoid a skateboard. ". . . but especially today. You wouldn't believe this week. We've been making polite conversation with one suspect after the other. They're all beginning to act like characters from one of the E. M. Forster novels I'm teaching. You know how Forster's main characters appear to be one thing on the outside, but on the inside they are something else, something a little twisted away from the ordinary. That also describes every member of the English department. During this semester, they all showed a polite collegiality to Les, if they showed anything. Now it turns out that Les was so intensely disliked that each of our professorial buddies had a minor motive for murdering him.

"At least you and Curt and Tony and I are not only innocents, but all of us were rather fond of Les, though I probably never showed it enough. Did I ever tell you how he saved me from embarrassment? It was a simple bit of advice that made a big difference. He told me to change my chalkboard erasing style, to start to erase up and down, vertically. It turned out that when I vigorously erased horizontally, from side to side, I put a lot of wiggle work into it and all the male students were making public, appreciative bun comments."

"Speaking of being fond of Les," Curley said, greeting us at the door, "I still have his library books. I told your colleagues, Mary Beth, that I would return them to the Buckeye for Les, sort of as my last tribute to him. Would 'the Buck stops here' be appropriate? I guess not. Here, give me your bagels." Curley relieved me of my bag and dumped its contents on a waiting plate. Jan exercised admirable control over her natural artistic homemaker's censorship and didn't rearrange a one. "I'm going to pay Les's fines and explain the situation," Curley continued to speak as he continued to dump bagels, "but I thought as long as you were coming over, you could look through the books to see if he made any notes or if a mysterious letter was stuck between the pages. I don't know. You're the ones looking for clues. But let's have some bacon and eggs first. As our mutual friend Stew has been heard to say, 'a boiled egg in the morning is hard to beat.'"

"It's better when he cracks it," laughed Tony.

"I'll ignore that," replied Janet, "But while you're in your Nick and Nora mode, I'm going to excuse myself. I have my own work to finish. I'm right in the middle of a rather intricate piece. I think it will be smashing when I'm through. I'll have you over to look at it, Mary Beth. Maybe you should come too, Tony. And I can drop 'hint, hint' signs all around it if you'd like me to, Mary Beth. It looks like you. Anyway, you know that I have a tin ear for detective work and the labyrinth of academic politics." Unconsciously placing a bagel and a cup of coffee on a small tray in the most artistically attractive arrangement possible-the exact opposite of Curley's serving style-she left the room. How does she do that? I wondered with admiration. I would have spilled the coffee, probably the bagel too.

Helping himself to bacon and eggs, Curt said, "Take the books home and peruse them." He added a friendly dig: "We ordinary scientists look at the pages; you English profs 'peruse' them. I'll pick them up later. Meanwhile, I do have some information from Seth. It's public information now. *The Repository* will probably carry a small article on it tomorrow. Abby turned in her preliminary report, I guess you nouveaux pros say the M.E.'s report, yesterday. The paperweight turns out to be a non-clue. McKenzie says it was used to hit Les after he was killed. If Les had been killed by a blow to the head, his heart would have stopped pumping. This is huge, Mary Beth, huge and negative. We know we don't know who killed Les. Now we don't know how he was killed either. Seth started to explain something to me about Les absorbing poison. As a scientist, I know that if he had been killed by a blow to the head and his heart had stopped pumping, he wouldn't have been able to absorb the poison." He stopped there. "But what I didn't know was, is that what they are looking at now? Are they thinking about a poison? Anyway, Seth thinks the paperweight was a ruse, a decoy clue, to draw the police away from the real clues. It didn't draw them very far away, but it did occupy some of the original detecting time."

Tony and Curt finished brunch discussing the non-significance of the paperweight. I stayed with them long enough to spread apple butter on my bagel (how Ohio can you get?) and drink my coffee and Tony's. Then I withdrew to Curt's study where I spent the next hour following his advice of perusing the pages of Les's library books. Quite a stack. It was obvious that Curt hadn't looked at them at all; they weren't from the Buck. Most of them were inter-library loans from the Library of Congress. A couple of them were reprints of studies written 40 and 50 years ago, telling of incidents distorted by the 'official' Eurocentric version of African history. What in the world would Les have wanted with them? His thesis is on the American writers Melville and Poe. Melville and Poe wrote in English even if some of our students do have problems understanding them! Most of these articles are about the French language and the authors who took "the French language away from the governing elite and gave it to the people." How could there be any use for these articles in his dissertation? He could be listing old sources, but this whole group of writings was exceedingly strange. I decided to ask Stew about it. He was working closely with Les and besides he had been very curious to know what books Les had borrowed. At least he would be interested.

As I leafed through the pages, they became stranger and stranger. Some of this stuff even sounded familiar. How could I be experiencing deja vu over articles I had never read? Had I been an anti-colonialist in a previous life? I knew I'd read or heard some of this material before. But where? I had just finished teaching a three-week segment on *A Passage to India*. E. M. Forster was certainly against the English colonialists he saw in India, but he doesn't lecture. He makes his point through story telling. I admired Forster's use of satire to put down the English colonialists, but these articles were almost diatribes. Somehow, whole sentences sounded familiar. The didactic style sounded familiar too. I couldn't have dreamt anything as arcane as some of the articles. And what were those scratch marks or hieroglyphics next to certain paragraphs? Curt was right though, other than the scratch marks, Les hadn't made any notes in the text.

I returned to the present social context. Like Scarlett O'Hara, I would think about my problems tomorrow. Curt and Tony seemed to be having a pleasant afternoon, discussing the murder, of course. They pointed out to me that everyone had an alibi. We three were O.K. Sally verified that Stew was at home. She's loyal and not the brightest bulb on the Christmas tree, but she would never lie. She's much too upright and uptight for that. Gary was in the clear, too. The librarians thought Gary was at the Buck just before the meeting, but couldn't swear to it. Not a problem for Gary. When Seth let him have an hour at his own desk in his own office, he had no trouble finding his computer-time receipt. He knew he had saved it. The receipt showed conclusively that he was buckled down. Tony and I, at the same time remembering Gary's attempt at a 'buck-eled' pun, started laughing hysterically. Curt went on patiently explaining in his science-for-idiots voice that Gary had been in a computer carrel from 2 until immediately before the department meeting that wasn't. His reasons for being on-line so long sounded just like Gary, too. His full-Gary reason? He had been at the Buck looking up some obscure note to one of Roberts Rules of Order that would permit him to use a technicality to keep Roger from voting.

And Roger was close to being saved by an unknown admirer. The administrative secretary had a long-time crush on him. She spent a great deal of her working day watching him, deciding what he was going to do next, what he was thinking, and, most importantly, how she could insert herself into those doings and thinkings. Monday was no different. She'd had her eye on him instead of her computer most of the afternoon, though she begged Seth not to include her Roger-obsession in any official testimony unless absolutely necessary. I don't see how it would be necessary to involve her as she couldn't testify to every minute of the day. Loomis was so close to the library that any 'bathroom break' would have given Roger enough time to do the deed.

Charlie was the only one without a verifiable alibi. But amateur detectives that we are, we figured that proved his innocence. Certainly if he was guilty, he would have prepared a good cover for his actions. But if he, too, had been blackmailed by Les, he had the same motive as Roger did and more unaccounted-for time.

We waved our goodbyes across the rooms to Janet who never had rejoined us, but who raised her bottle of water in acknowledgement. We had all agreed to meet at my house in a week for our regular Sunday brunch. It is funny that none of us calls it a regular weekly brunch. We all follow the conceit of re-inventing our date each week. I guess we like to think we are free-spirited, spontaneous friends; none of us wants to be in the kind of rut easily generated by small town living.

Tony and I greeted the three Johnsons who were coming up Purley's driveway as we were going down it. The minute we saw the Johnsons, Tony and I emailed each other eye messages. We knew that because they were new in town and on campus, the Johnsons were having a hard time adjusting. He is African-American. She is Asian. And they had adopted a Romanian toddler, who looked about the age of Curt and Janet's youngest. The little girl was happily blowing on a silver whistle. Those S.O.S. whistles had been put to some good use. As soon as the Johnsons were in the house, Tony and I concurred that super-mentor Curt had lost no time in more than filling Les's shoes.

Domesticated for a change, the two of us lazily spent what was left of the afternoon reading the Sunday papers. What a pleasure. We didn't even pretend to work. Even though I had taken home some of Les's library books that nagged at me-well, I would really concentrate on them tomorrow. That night we ended up sleeping on the floor at my house. We were having such a good time in bed that we pulled each other on to the floor and decided to pull down the duvet and stay there.

Maybe it was the slightly different bedroom floor environment, but early in the morning, I woke up, alert. Aware. I remembered. I knew where I had seen some of those phrases that bothered me at Purley's. I'd read almost those exact sentences that had bothered me yesterday in an article Stew ostentatiously left lying around because he was so proud to have had an article published by the Modern Language Association in the *PMLA*. Coincidence? Coincidence might act as strong novelistic machinery. It can make a plot move. But this was life, and Seth had warned me that good detectives don't believe in coincidences.

The *PMLA* piece was one of those articles based on Stew's dissertation, as was everything he published. It was based on the original grad school research he did. He supposedly did. The motive for murder couldn't have been Stew concerned about plagiarism, could it? No, that was an idea not worth its kosher salt.

I couldn't help playing with it though, and I know why.

Professor Silverman explained it in a recent interview. She said that we of the academic set spend our days in libraries, classrooms, and archives. Given the scant opportunity for stimulation, a literary kidnapping or plagiarism offers the only taste of salacious activity many of us experience in a school year. Well, I seem to have a better sex life than she does, but still, I couldn't stop thinking about the problems involved.

I visualized those letters scratched in the margins. That wasn't enough. I got up and looked through the oldest volume again. At first the marks had looked like Tolkien's Elvish writings, but looking with my reading glasses on ($15 a pair at Renny's drugstore), I could see that the pencilings were actual letters. 'W.J.' or sometimes a simple 'w.' Could Les have been unobtrusively marking passages that had been plagiarized by W. Stewart Jones? Did all of Stew's renown, and no matter how much we teased him, he did have a reputation, was all of that based on a plagiarized dissertation? If Les had found that out, I'm sure Stew would have wanted to kill him. Would have wanted to and could have. If exposed, Stew would never be able to get a job in any kind of a college, school, or academic setting again. It's a question if he would be able to get any kind of a job any place if this thieving came out. But still, murder?

Was I getting obsessive about Les and blackmail? He couldn't have been blackmailing everyone in Midfield's English department. Could he? For what? Did he plan to buy a whole fleet of Cannondales? Did he just like to have power over his tenured 'superiors'?

Tony and I had to see Seth.

Chapter Twenty-one

*Mordre wol out, certen,
it wol not faille*

Chaucer, *"The Prioress's Tale"*

❧

Roger was elated to be an emergency substitute for me on Monday morning. He was happy to be in front of a class again and happy to be playing even a peripheral role in the important work of finding Les's killer. Tony had a little more trouble finding someone who could do his 'dirty' work for him. But easy-going Boss Bob was happy to give him the morning off. The last customer who had complained that again his brakes didn't work got short shrift from repairman Tony. Tony snapped: if he didn't like the way he'd fixed the brakes, he would just make the horn honk louder. Bob thought Tony's taking the morning off would provide a nice cooling down period for all concerned.

So Tony was bright eyed, and I was reasonably alert as

we greeted Seth outside of the police station at 7:30 am. It was only a few steps to Seth's office, but those few steps took time because we couldn't walk by Deputy Miller or Amos Hershberger, who was there handing in his Campus Patrol report, without exchanging the usual Midfield pleasantries. I aimed my generic "nice day" at both men. Miller replied with a hearty "10-4." And Amos turned a flushing red, flattering to me if not to his complexion. I'm beginning to enjoy the way we do business here.

I had the two pertinent library books with me and a stack of published monographs and offprints. At first I talked too fast for Seth to understand anything except that we were giving him a lot of homework assignments to read. It took him a while to decipher that Tony and I thought we had some important, break-through information.

"Slow down. In your case, a blueberry muffin and a cup of high caffeine coffee might even calm you a bit. You've been in a perpetual state of readiness for a week now, Mary Beth. Take one day at a time. Sit down. Relax. Sometime even your thoughts need a little organization."

Did he mean especially my thoughts?

"I try to take one day at a time, Seth, but lately several days have been attacking me at once. I'll try to go slowly. Here's the full story." I added the books and papers I was carrying to Seth's seemingly permanent accumulation on his desk. "Yesterday Tony and I were with the prof the kids call Curley Purley . . .."

"Yes, Curt Perlis . . .."

I ignored Seth's identification acknowledgment, " ....
Perlis, Les's mentor and friend, still had some library books
that Les hadn't returned. A big stack. Most of the books
were what you would expect from the burgeoning field of
post colonial lit."

"I think it's a field that has already burgeoned, Mary
Beth," quipped Tony.

Was nobody going to let me finish?

"But two of them were rather strange. These two," I
pointed to the materials starting to slip off of Seth's desk.
"They are both by the same author. Brandon B. Claven. No
one I've ever heard of. But that's not what's so strange.
These are reprints of books, studies that were done 50 and
40 years ago. No one writing a literary dissertation today
would use such old references except for historical docu-
mentation. You know, if someone wanted to give historical
heft by saying, 'Fifty years ago people believed that all
language was ingrained, etc. . . . ' but Les really wouldn't
need the books. His dissertation is about Melville and Poe.
The articles in these books have nothing to do with
American Lit. When I began looking at the passages he had
marked, I realized that in many cases I had read the exact
sentences at some other time."

"But Seth, there's more." I opened a book to a marked
page and put my photocopy of Stew's latest *PMLA* article
next to it. You didn't have to be a quantum physicist or
an English major to recognize that Stew's sentence
beginning with "The French Raj response to the official

Eurocentric version of African history" was copied from the article. In Stew's next paragraph the introductory sentence, "'a discussion of those who took the French language away from the elite governing class and gave it to the people" that had been plagiarized from the same article was foot-noted all right. It was foot-noted and attributed to Stew's own dissertation.

While Seth examined the documents, I brought my narrative to its climax: "Then around 4 a.m., long after Tony and I had fallen asleep, I woke up suddenly. You know how your mind keeps working while you are asleep?"

"Sometimes I do all of my best thinking that way," Tony laughed.

I was too involved with the explanation of my own epiphany to comment. "What woke me up," I explained "was the realization that the strange markings next to those familiar passages weren't Elvish chicken tracks, but rather initials. If you'll look closely, you can see that they say 'WJ' and sometimes just 'w'. Sometimes they were exclamation points or inverted exclamation points."

Seth turned the top book around to examine the marginal marks."Of course," he murmured while licking his finger to turn the pages, "those inverted exclamation marks are Margarita M's Spanish influence on Les. He must have borrowed punctuation marks from her for added emphasis. That's why you didn't recognize what they were when you first saw them, Mary Beth. The rest of the markings seem obvious now. Les used Stew's initials to mark every original idea that Stew had plagiarized. But he wanted to keep his findings as his secret weapon against Stew; that's the why and wherefore of the 'w's instead of 'Stew' next to each example."

"Sure. Once I connected the exclamation points to paragraphs about colonialism, I started to think of Stew. It was all too clear. I looked at the 'w's again. Les's code wasn't very hard to break. Most of the 'w's' were next to lines that had sounded familiar to me. And we all know that Stew's name is W. Stewart Jones, though no one seems to know or care, what the 'W' stands for."

"This is the first real motivation we've found. Seth, in case you haven't dealt with academic plagiarism before-it's usually dealt with within the college community-there's no time period after which it's O.K. to copy some living person's work."

"Mary Beth, remember? We have newspapers right here in Midfield. *The Repository* even uses wire services. I've read about *The New York Times'* problems. I know what's been going on with Doris Kearns Goodwin and that fellow Ambrose, both of them being accused of plagiarism. I'm pretty sure now that the argument Les and Stew were having when they came into the lunchroom on Monday wasn't only about two historians. It was about these two historians who plagiarized."

"You're right, Seth, I'm sorry. And in a less well-known case, a California Law School Dean just got kicked out for plagiarizing from a 14 year old *Encyclopedia Britannica*! A

Law School Dean." I shook my head in disbelief. "That
was really dumb. Everyone refers to the *Britannica*. At
least Stew chose to copy an author who even most academics had never heard of or ever paid any attention to-
until Les started to write his dissertation using Stew's
research as a partial base. I don't know how long plagiarism
has been the supreme academic crime, but I do know that
conceits such as the research imperative, intellectual property, and academic originality date back to the 18th century.
That means that plagiarism has been some kind of a crime
for more than two centuries. We warn students against it
every semester. Stew can't use, 'I didn't know what I was
doing' as an excuse."

Seth stopped me with a knowing smile, "Your academic
friend Doris Kearns Goodwin seems to be using it."

I persisted with my explanation whether it was necessary
or not: "Midfield's entire faculty recognizes the potential
for students to plagiarize and we're always double checking
their papers against articles on the Internet. The software
for detecting plagiarism has been available for a few years
now and we make good use of it. We monitor student
papers with Turnitin, a leading California company. With
their help, the window of opportunity for intellectual cheats
is closing fast. The University of Virginia just dismissed 45
students caught by another computer program. That'll be a
lesson for potential student cheaters. But here at the
College, we never think of plagiarism in conjunction with
our professional peers. Now we have to.

"It's not just the dissertation that was plagiarized, though that's enough to get Stew or anyone kicked out. Out. Out. It's that Stew has published about 20 papers on the same subject. They all say pretty much the same thing. But they are all plagiarizations, all based on the work of others. He has stolen every paper he's written or given at a conference. I'm sure as he saw it, when-if-Les confronted him, he had no choice. Les's discovery had to be the death knell for Stew or for Les."

"Whoa. Whoa, Mary Beth. You've given me a lot of fodder to digest here. You sure have a lot of ideas here, some of them good ones. But they are all based on your and Tony's deciphering of some inscriptions I haven't even seen yet. How about leaving those two books and Stew's articles with me and coming back here after your classes this afternoon? Need I add, please do not tell any of your colleagues or friends, that includes Dr. and Mrs. Perlis, that includes our own M.E., your buddy Abby. Don't tell anyone what you suspect. Don't even hint about it to Margarita Berenguer."

My slight chagrin at Seth's tone was accompanied by a wave of compassion at the mention of M & M's name again. Margarita might finally get that "closure" she had so tearfully begged for.

I was so over-stimulated by our new evidence and the good chance Les's murder might be solved that my freshman comp went by in a psychedelic swirl. In my E. M. Forster class, I found myself dwelling on Forster's attitudes toward colonialism in *A Passage to India* where he highlights the falsity implicit in the lives of the Anglo-Indians he deplores. I taught both classes on a high, finished talking to the last student lying in wait for me outside of my office, pulled Tony away from his computer where he had been busy entering a series of engineer's cabalistic symbols, and managed to be back in Seth's office by 3:30.

Seth didn't bother with preliminaries. Tony was just starting the job of folding his long frame into a small wooden chair when Seth, skipping greetings, announced, "You're right about the notes in these two books. No question about it. You know how some people are always bemoaning that opportunity never comes? That's 'cause they don't recognize opportunity when it does knock, but I do and I think this is it. The letters 'w' and 'wj,' and the exclamation points all show up at relevant paragraphs. I had plenty of time to compare some of those marked paragraphs with Stew's monographs you gave me. Word for word transcriptions. These sentences and paragraphs definitely provide a motive. More, they'll be the second step in the deconstruction of Stew's alibi. Like that, Mary Beth? Deconstruction of an alibi? I'd better get away from your English department soon. I'm learning to walk the walk and talk the talk."

Not waiting for my answer, he shrugged, "I've already taken care of the first step in breaking down his alibi. In fact, I went back over each person's alibi, double checking details," Seth said, continuing with his amazingly calm monologue. "When I met with Stew's wife Sally again, she repeated that she had seen Stew come in at 1:00 and leave the house at 4:30. This time around I asked the right questions. As a result, what I learned is that she didn't see him anytime between his coming and going. Not once. He could have walked out the back door at 2:30, shot up half the town, come back in at 4 and ostentatiously gone out again at 4:30. So I know that Stew does not have an alibi for the time when Les and Krypto were murdered. What I didn't have was a motivation or actual method for the murder. It looks like you two have supplied the motivation, but all we know about the method is that Les was not killed with the paper-weight. At the crime scene we could see immediately what forensics showed later: there simply wasn't enough blood for the paperweight to have been the murder weapon. It had to have been used as some kind of an afterthought, possibly by a murderer in a panic. We've assumed all along that the perpetrator is inexperienced and . . . ."

A knock on the door interrupted our meeting. It was Deputy Dwayne Miller, baseball cap backward, I noticed. How quickly life returned to normal for everyone but Les. With a snappy "10-5," implying he was relaying a message, Dwayne announced that Dr. Abby MacKenzie had arrived. "Want to see her now, Chief?" he almost saluted.

"Of course." Seth got up to greet Abby who walked in as Deputy Dwayne was asking the question.

Tony and I wanted to stay, but felt that police decorum required us to leave. This wasn't our Abby dropping by the office to chat, but rather Dr. Abby McKenzie M.E., there on official business. Fortunately, Seth gave us a left-handed signal, a command to remain seated, as he used his right to pull up a small folding chair for Abby. Abby is taller than I am, but she's flexible and graceful even when she's not swimming, so she had no trouble twisting into the chair to join us in the rather small office. It wasn't even 48 hours ago that a different foursome (Tony and I, Stew and Seth) had crowded into that same office for Chinese take-out. Abby ignored the palpable emotions that surrounded us to greet us with her clear, still smile. But even our unfazeable Abby recognized the difficulty of the situation by skipping her usual salutation of, "Hey, good to see you." Instead she waved a manuscript of papers and went straight to her purpose for being there, "I have some news I wanted to deliver personally, Seth."

"All of those pages?" I complained. "Abby-dear, give it to us in a nutshell."

"Mary Beth, prescient punner. Listen, these papers are my final M.E. report. The tests show conclusively that Les died of an allergic reaction. You'll want to read each test and results, but I can give you a three word summation: An allergic reaction."

"An allergic reaction?" I couldn't believe it.

"Yes, to peanut protein." She turned to me, "So you see why I was so startled when you said give us the report in a nutshell? Prescient punner, indeed. Les must have ingested it without knowing it. We all know he never would get near a peanut; he was so allergic and so conscious of his allergies.

We believe that a drop of peanut butter was dissolved in minute amounts of peanut oil, and then introduced into the wine bottle. With his allergies it wouldn't take much to produce an anaphylactic reaction."

"What are you saying? Do you think Stew or someone forced the peanut solution on him or seduced him into eating it?"

"Yes," Seth took control of the conversation. "I'm betting on 'seduced.' Someone lured Les into drinking it. That's what all the wine business was about. Stew-or someone-offered Les a wine tasting of some rare, at least rare to Les, wine."

Tony raced on with the idea. "Mary Beth, remember on our wine tour when Duke Cherkowski told us that a colleague had been there asking about wine additives? I'll bet it was Stew. Les would have been such a sucker for something like that. And he had no nose. Anything could have been poured into that bottle."

"It wasn't 'anything,' Tony," Abby patiently explained. "The autopsy revealed symptoms-swelling of the larynx and edema of the lungs-that are entirely consistent with anaphylactic shock " She looked at our puzzled faces and added, "That's a severe, in this case, really severe-fatal-systemic immune reaction."

"I know the term, Abby." Seth bristled a bit. "Though this is the first time I've thought of it as connected with the method. It fits and even helps to explain the inconsistent evidence. If the glasses and bottle were tainted, no wonder they are gone, but the perp didn't bother to take the cork.

He must have known that you couldn't get finger or palm prints from it."

Seth held the floor: "We did get blood work-ups in from the State Lab. They were inconclusive. No corroborating details. All we know so far is that none of Les's blood was found on anyone's briefcase. But there were definitely some suspicious spots on Stew's case even if they weren't Les's blood. We used to work with the F.B.I. and often had to wait a year to process DNA. Now in just this short time, we're expecting the B.C.I's DNA report."

My explanation, Abby's report, and Seth's response had taken some time. My wrist alarm, set to remind me to start dinner went off. Start dinner? That was in another lifetime! It was 5:30, past closing time for most Midfield businesses, but the sheriff's office was energized and working at full, if limited, capacity. Almost as if my wrist alarm sounding the time set them off, the phone started to ring, the copy machine whirred incriminatory copies of marked pages, and the Fax machine spit out information. Because of the size of Seth's office, the Fax almost landed in his lap, but he intercepted the sheets mid-air with a practiced hand. One of them was the DNA report.

"That's it! We have a match. That's Krypto's blood on Stew's briefcase. Stew or, to be fair, someone carrying Stew's briefcase had to have been in the room around the time of death."

"It couldn't be. Stew? Killing Les? Even killing Krypto?"

"Yes, Mary Beth," Tony repeated, "'Even killing Krypto.' Stew would be out of a job even if it's 'just' Krypto we're talking about. Remember those two Hispanic police officers in New York who were dismissed after being linked to the death of 'Fred the beagle,' a station house mascot? Killing a pet is a serious crime."

"There's no question about it," Seth interrupted Tony's legal history lesson. "Listen to this report. The BCI turned the blood sample over to an animal DNA expert. He said the drops from briefcase C10-blind coding for W. Stewart Jones's case-matched Krypto's DNA in all ten key points of analysis. The blood could have only come from Krypto. It must have splattered on Stew's briefcase when Krypto and Les were killed at approximately the same time."

"This is so odd," I exclaimed. "It was Stew who told me that Krypto's name came from the Greek for 'hidden' or 'secret,' and it's that decoded secret of hers that's the clincher in solving this crime."

"You're right, Mary-Babe, and I know you'll hate me for being corny at a time like this, but there would be something so fitting in yon literary prof giving voice to that line from Macbeth, 'Out damned spot! Out, I say!'"

Chapter Twenty-two

*<Intellectual> Debt is a prolific mother of folly
and of crime.*

Benjamin Disraelli, 1834

≈●

Efficient in everything he does, Seth knows how to take maximum advantage of his small office: He swiveled his chair, reached into his file cabinet and retrieved the Midfield College English department file. He had a page for each one of us showing our daily class schedules and likely whereabouts when not in class. My sheet was upside down, but I haven't been reading essays and stories to classes for nothing all of these years. My upside down reading skills are superb. I could clearly see the three blue blocks marked 'swim' on my weekly sheet. And it looked as if Monday nights were blocked out for my regular dinner with Tony at Our Place. Who wants to be known as being that predictable? Besides, I don't like that kind of Big

Brothering. I suppose I'm lucky he hadn't chartered my menstrual cycle. On the positive side, a quick glance at the file was all Seth needed to locate Stew.

"Stew is probably at home right now," Seth informed the three of us. "I'd like to walk in unannounced and I wouldn't object to your joining me."

Abby emphatically refused Seth's invitation, "Look. I don't belong here. I don't want to belong here. I belong in the Wellness Center. Even the morgue would be better than going over to Stew's . . . to do what? To accuse a friend?" Abby worried about me too. "Mary Beth, are you sure you want to be there? Is a DNA match with Krypto's blood enough proof? Please don't say anything until you're sure. You're not a western rider like I am, but I know you'll understand me when I advise you not to squat with your spurs on!"

She turned to Tony, "That's from Will Rogers, Tony. You can put it in your book."

Then with an affectionately restraining hand on my arm, she turned to leave, "Call me at the Center. I'll be there until noon."

Tony and I looked at each other. We were surprised that Seth had included us. But our exchange of glances signaled a determination to see it through. We had worked hard on solving the murders; we felt strongly about Les and Krypto, too. We weren't about to quit now.

We left the office in Seth's car with Amos following us in his alpaca-smelling truck, now pressed into service as a police vehicle. Placing a sheriff's star on the dashboard, Amos proudly and efficiently transformed his farm truck into a police wagon. Amos is such a good guy. He even phoned in a '10-76' en route to cheer up Deputy Dwayne Miller who had to stay back on Main Street to mind the store. I do have to fix-up Amos with Abby.

Stew's house is just a short distance from the Police Station. Everything in Midfield is just a short distance from the Police station. Everything in Midfield is just a short distance from Stew's house. I was more nervous than I thought.

Tony and I stood behind Seth as he knocked at the door. Stew answered. Thank goodness. I couldn't face Sally. Not now.

Stew took one long look that encompassed Seth and his back-up, Amos, waiting in the truck. He knew. As if to keep that knowledge at bay, to ward off the inevitable, he started talking, talking, talking.

"I knew I heard you going, 'Knock. Knock.' I was going to say, 'Who's there?' . . . that's a good straight line-You know, a straight line, the shortest distance between two jokes, which reminds me of a good one that came in my email today . . . ." He wouldn't stop. Maybe he couldn't stop.

"We're not here to tell jokes, Stew. This isn't a social call," Seth said quietly.

"You mean I'm being considered as a prime suspect?" Stew retorted, slowing down long enough to lead us into his study. But once seated in his well worn favorite armchair

(Sally had redecorated the rest of the room, I noted), he carried on mid-story. He still couldn't stop talking.

"Am I a prime suspect or the prime suspect? Am I A, B, C, or D on your list, Seth? You know that we academicians like everything and everyone to be graded." He looked round the room. "You're certainly responding to my questions with a dead silence, if you'll excuse the expression."

Seth looked Stew straight in the eyes. "These delaying tactics aren't going to help you, Stew," he said in that same quiet voice.

In contrast, Stew's voice was too loud. He responded so suddenly, with sentences that came so rapidly, they overflowed with words: "I had the perfect crime. But you know what they say, 'if you want to hear God laugh, tell her your plans.' And I didn't even give a hint to Duke Chirkowski when I researched it at his Midfield Crick Winery. Cozy name, isn't it?

"Such a perfect set-up with Les and his allergies. Boy, did I pre-meditate on it. Les's allergies might have been a pain to him. Hearing about them was a pain to everyone. But they were a godsend to me. If it hadn't been for that damn Krypto nosing around. I always pretended to like her, but I didn't. I hate her as much as Charlie does. More. He wouldn't have been able to kill her.

What was she doing in Loomis Hall anyway? What were Mary Beth and her whatsisname doing there? No one is ever in Loomis before the regular department meeting. Most Monday afternoons you could kill a whole comp class there and you wouldn't have a witness. Not 'til those newcomers showed up. They don't understand tradition."

He turned. It was almost a plea, "You don't understand anything, Mary Beth."

Seth stopped Stew's outpouring and partial confession to read him his rights.

"You're under arrest, Stew Jones."

"W. Stewart Jones, Ph.D.," Stew murmured, correcting him.

"You're under arrest, Dr. W. Stewart Jones, for the murders of Les Delaney and the dog Krypto. I am now going to give you notice of your Constitutional Rights. I am a Police Officer. I warn you that anything you say will be used in a Court of Law against you; that you have an absolute right to remain silent; that you have the right to advice of a lawyer before and the presence of a lawyer here with you during questioning; and that if you cannot afford a lawyer, one will be appointed for you for free before any questioning, if you desire.

"I want to add that if you decide to answer questions now without a lawyer present, you will still have the right to stop answering at any time until you talk to a lawyer. Do you understand, Professor Jones?"

"Of course I understand," Stew brushed off the Miranda-izing. He wouldn't be stopped. "And I was afraid of Krypto, too, because she probably knew how much I hated her. They say dogs can sense those things. And she was always so damn smart. I knew if I left her alive she'd be a witness against me."

Seth's interruption was authoritative. "She's a witness against you in death, Stew. Her DNA is an exact match to a drop of blood on your briefcase."

"I knew that damn dog would be the one to convict me. Though I almost gave myself away at the beginning when your Deputy Dwayne claimed that fibers from Gary's rug were evidence against me."

Stew's smile at himself was one of approval. "I knew with 100% accuracy that the murderer-me-left his briefcase near the door of Gary's office and did not bring it into the office itself last Monday. When you showed up, Seth, and stopped Dwayne's accusation, wow, that was just in time to keep me from blurting out something incriminating, like 'No way was my briefcase on Gary's rug'."

Stew turned so that he created an intimate space with Seth, talking one on one. "But how could that blood have gotten all the way to my briefcase at the door? Of course, that damn dog jumping up and down squirted his damn blood every place. It's just like that bitch of a dog."

"Stew, are you admitting to the murder of the dog Krypto?"

"Yes. And, as you darn well know, to the murder of that dog Les Delaney too. What a sucker. First I thought I'd just put a drop or so of peanut oil in any bottle of wine that I was going to pass around the department. Then, bless the anxious mothers that started the website on peanut allergies, I discovered that the oil alone wouldn't do it. In fact, theoretically, anyone allergic to peanuts should find peanut oil completely safe because the allergic culprit is the protein content. Who would've guessed? So I had to put a dab of peanut butter in the bottle, too, and had to do it for Les only. He had absolutely no nose, couldn't tell what he was drinking. But anyone else might have noticed something more than a little off about a bottle of wine that smelled like peanuts."

At this point, Sally appeared in the doorway with a welcoming smile and an even more welcoming tray of coffee and cookies. As she entered Stew's study ready to banter a bit, she realized that something was different. The heavy discomfort of the situation was palpable. She looked startled, automatically started to pass the tray, stopped, placed the tray precisely in the center of the end table, and sat down heavily.

I kicked Tony who was sitting next to me on the couch. The cookies were freshly baked. We could all smell what normally would have been a mouth-watering aroma. They were peanut butter cookies.

Sally noticed the kick. She visibly gathered her strength to get out of the arm chair.

"I think a good lawyer can get me off," Stew continued without acknowledging Sally's entrance or hurried exit. "In a way, it was self-defense. Yes, that's it. It was self-defense. He was blackmailing me, you know."

Tony whispered to me, "That's the final how and why of the Cannondale specialty bike Bob told us Les had ordered."

I shushed him. Stew's recitation of what he considered logical reasoning was going on, "During my somewhat distinguished career, I've used information I've borrowed from some people in my field. Actually, it was a little more than information. At times, I even borrowed their words. But now I've got Doris Kearns Goodwin on my side. She did a little borrowing, too. She didn't call it 'borrowing,' though. I think she called it 'a failure to adequately attribute some passages.'"

Stew intercepted potential questions with his endless rationalizations which morphed into preparations of his defense: "How could I have been sure he would have an anaphylactic reaction?". Shutting out his semi-hysterical monologue with my own thoughts, I realized that if Les had exposed Stew, others would have come forth who could verify or give similar testimony against him. This would have resulted in the McCollege's first legal action to have a professor removed from a teaching position. The school certainly would have gotten national publicity about it. And it wouldn't have been positive publicity either. Everyone would have wanted Stew out of there. The case would have been important in its own right, but now that the Goodwin and Steven Ambrose scandals have made the academy's dirty little secret public, now that we know it's not just the students who plagiarize, Stew's sins would have been added to the bonfire of reputations.

Seth was talking quietly to Stew. Tony turned to me,

"It's like your epiphany, Mary Beth. Suddenly everything fits together: Midfield College, Stew, my Bartlett's *Better Quotations*."

"Mary Beth, here's my missing thief. Remember Saturday night when we were trying to fit all the suspects into Thomas de Quincy's quotation? 'If once a man indulges himself in murder, very soon he comes to think little of robbing; and from robbing he comes next to drinking and Sabbath-breaking, and from that to incivility and procrastination.' We were almost there. We almost solved the crimes then."

"You're right again, Tony." I was as excited as he was. "We were missing that one piece of the puzzle, Stew as the thief of intellectual property. We know Stew's motivation for murder was Les's threat to disclose those repeated plagiarisms of his."

"My quotation. My turn, Mary Babe. That threat of the disclosure of Stew's robbery of intellectual property makes it easy to paraphrase de Quincy's 'Murder as one of the fine arts,' and to do it right this time: If once Stew indulges himself in murder, very soon Stew comes to think little of robbing; and from robbing we come next to Charlie's drinking and Roger's Sabbath-breaking, and from that to Gary's incivility and . . ." He put his arm around me, "Mary Beth's procrastination."

"It's all academic, my dear."

Midfield Campus College

17 November 2004

Dear Friend of the College:

These terrible events of last week, centered in the Department of English, surprised and saddened us all. Such critical events as the death of Teaching Assistant Les Delaney and the subsequent arrest of the allegedly guilty party by our good friend and fellow citizen of Midfield, Sheriff Seth Yoder, mark a significant change and challenge to all of us.

One of the immediate changes is in staffing of the English Department. The resignation of long-time faculty member Dr. W. Stewart Jones has been accepted with regret. In a related development, the search committee is in process of looking for his replacement (see advert in the next two issues of the *Chronicle of Higher Education*). Dr. Jones is leaving private education to relocate to a state facility.

The only other modification resulting from last week's incidents is that peanut butter will no longer be a staple at meals. We hope that students will not act unfavorably to this change. Because of the solemnity of the occasion, we are asking for no protest meetings
.

I remind you that we have carefully nurtured, academically talented students, who now will be required to register all food allergies with Dr. McKenzie at the Student Wellness Center. We are also blessed with outstanding faculty, staff, and alumni; a balanced budget; generous donors; and an always inspiring campus in the heartland of this great country.

Midfield Campus College

I would like to close on a personal note: I will, as will all of you, miss our mascot Krypto, but we will continue to move ahead to the future with pride and confidence because it is my belief that the small, liberal arts college and, in particular, Midfield Campus College, is the greatest achievement of the human mind.

To continue and enhance Midfield's achievements, remember that our Capital Fund Campaign "Commitment to Excellence" is now underway. Your commitment, your contribution from $25.00 to $2500.00 can be sent in the enclosed envelope.

Sincerely,

Dr. Fairchild Bender, President

Dr. Fairchild Bender, President

About the Author

Photography: Linda R. Hengst, Director, Ohioana Library Assoc.

Dr. Audrey Lavin knows the college scene. She has taught in English Departments at colleges similar to Midfield Campus College, colleges where murders may or may not have occurred.

She also has been a faculty member at highly ranked universities and colleges, such as Ohio's Case Western Reserve U. (where she received her Ph.D.) and the College of Wooster. As a Fulbright Professor, she taught two years in Spain and continued to enliven pedagogy and discourse as a Visiting Professor at universities in 12 other countries from Colombia to Zambia.

Dr. Lavin's essays and critical studies have appeared in *The CEA Forum, College English,* various *E-Journals, the Journal of Popular Culture, Midstream, Ocean, Romance Notes,* and *Studies in English.* She has published in even more obscure learned journals in Chili, Russia, and Spain. *Eloquent Blood* is her fourth book.

When not teaching, Lavin writes and bird watches in Canton, Ohio, where she lives with her consultant husband Carl. They have four children, four children-in-law, and eleven grandchildren.